CAPTAIN HENRY GALLANT

H. Peter Alesso

THE HENRY GALLANT SAGA

Midshipman Henry Gallant in Space © 2013

Lieutenant Henry Gallant © 2014

Henry Gallant and the Warrior © 2015

Commander Henry Gallant © 2016

Captain Henry Gallant © 2019

Other Novels by H. Peter Alesso

Captain Hawkins © 2016

Dark Genius © 2017

Youngblood © 2018

CAPTAIN HENRY GALLANT

H. Peter Alesso

© 2019 H. Peter Alesso

This is a work of fiction. All characters, dialogue, and events portrayed in this book are fictional, and any resemblance to real people or incidents is purely coincidental.

VSL Publications
Pleasanton, CA 94566

Edition 1.00

ISBN-13: 9781077670242

∞

Not everyone who helps you,
is a friend.

Not everyone who hinders you,
is an enemy.

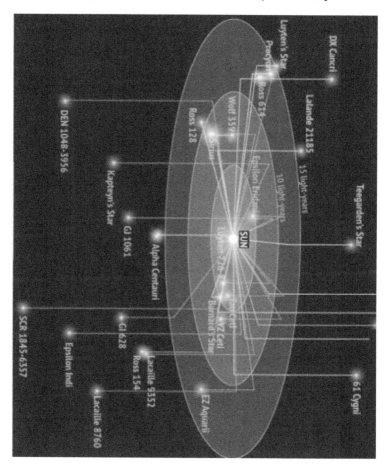

Figure 1: Stars Surrounding the Solar System

United Planets Home Fleet

1st Fleet – Fleet Admiral George Forsyth Collingsworth

4 Dreadnoughts –
Conqueror, Colossus, Defiant, Superb
4 Battlecruisers –
Achilles, Agamemnon, Arduous, Audacious
4 Spacecraft Carriers –
Arc Royal, Eagle, Hermes, Lexington
24 Cruisers
48 Destroyers
Stealth Recon – *Invidia*
72 Auxiliary Support Ships

UP Fleet in the Ross Star System

3rd Fleet - Vice Admiral Simon L. Graves
4 Dreadnought –
Vanguard, Valiant, Vanguard, Victory
4 Battlecruisers –
Indefatigable, Indomitable, Inflexible, Invincible
4 Spacecraft Carriers –
Constellation, Courageous, Glorious, Saratoga
24 Cruisers
48 Destroyers
Stealth Recon – *Warrior*
48 Auxiliary Support Ships

2nd Marine Division - Brigadier General William 'Bulldog' McIntyre

Headquarters Battalion
2nd Marine Regiment
4th Marine Regiment

6th Marine Regiment

8th Marine Regiment

10th Tank Battalion

12th Artillery Battalion

16nd Reconnaissance Company –
   Captain James Steward

20th SeaBee Construction Battalion

Titan Fleet in the Ross Star System - Admiral Zzey

6 Dreadnought

6 Battlecruisers

6 Spacecraft Carriers – *Vampiri, Wwrath*

96 Cruisers

288 Destroyers

288 Auxiliary Support Ships

CHAPTER 1

Streak Across the Sky

Cold night air smacked Rob Ryan in the face as he stepped out of the *Liftoff* bar—a favorite haunt of pilots. He was still weaving his way through the parking terminal looking for his single-seat jet-flyer when a familiar face appeared at his elbow.

Grabbing his arm, his friend said, "You shouldn't fly. Let me give you a ride."

Ryan straightened to his full six-two height and shrugged off his friend's hand.

"I'm fine," he said, swiping a lock of unkempt brown hair out of his eyes.

"Don't be pigheaded. There's a difference between self-reliance and foolishness."

He pushed past his friend. "Nonsense. I fly better when I'm . . . mellow."

As he left his buddy behind, he noticed a young woman who had come out of the bar after him. He had spent the past hour eyeing this smokin' hot redhead, but she had been with somebody. Now she was heading out on her own. She glanced at him and quickened her pace.

A thought penetrated the fog in his mind.

I'll show her.

At his Cobra 777 jet-flyer, he zipped up his pressure suit, buckled into the cockpit, and pulled on his AI neural interface—all the while imagining a wild take-off that would wow the redhead.

He jockeyed his jet along the taxiway onto the runway. When the turbo launch kicked in, the black-and-chrome jet spewed a cloud of exhaust and dust across the strip. He jammed the throttle all the way in and gave a whoop of pure joy at the roar and explosive thrust of the machine. The exhilaration—a primitive, visceral feeling—increased by the second, along with his altitude and speed. His love of speed was only matched by his almost unhealthy fascination with flying machines—too fast was never fast enough.

For a few seconds, his mind flashed back to his very first flight. The thrill only lasted a few minutes before the mini flyer spun out and crashed. Without a word, his father picked him up and sat him back down in the seat, restarting the engine with a wink and a grin. Clearest of all was the memory of his father's approval as he took off again and soared higher and faster than before.

Now he sliced through the crisp night air in a military jet that had his name engraved on the side. He ignited an extra thruster to drive the engine even hotter. Riding the rush of adrenaline, he pulled back on the stick to pull the nose up. Atmospheric flying was different than being in space, and for him, it had a sensual rhythm all its own. As he reached altitude, he pulled a tight loop and snapped the jet inverted, giving himself a bird's-eye view of the ground below.

But instead of reveling in admiration as expected, he found himself fighting for control against a powerful shockwave as a Scorpion 699 jet blew past him. The blast of its fuel exhaust was nothing compared to the indignation and shame that burned his face.

It was the redhead.

Damn. She's good.

His pulse raced as he came to full alert. Determined to pursue her, he angled the ship across air traffic lanes, breaking every safety regulation in the book. Instinctively his eyes scanned the horizon and the edges around him, watching for threats or other machines that might interfere with his trajectory. Pinwheeling in a high-G turn, he felt the crush of gravity against his chest, yet still, his hand on the throttle urged ever more speed from the machine.

He lost track of the Scorpion in the clouds, and in mere seconds she maneuvered behind him. He tried to shake her using every evasive maneuver he had learned in his fighter training but couldn't do it.

His eyes roamed the sky, watching for potential dangers. The night sky was dark, but several landmarks lit up the ground below him. Earth's capital, Melbourne, glowed with activity to the north; a mountain range stretched across the horizon 50 km to the west, and an airport lay to the south at the edge of the ocean.

As he scanned the skyline, he noticed a radio-telescope antenna. Impulsively he dove toward it, the Scorpion on his tail.

At the last moment, the redhead broke pursuit to avoid the antenna, but in a moment of reckless folly, Ryan crashed through the flimsy wire mesh, no more substantial to his Cobra than a wisp of cloud.

"That'll need a patch," he chuckled.

But once more, the Scorpion blew by him. He watched it roar away as if he were in slow motion. As the redhead curved back toward him for another pass, he gritted his teeth in frustration. With thrusters already at max burn, he punched the afterburner to create his own shock wave and turned head-on into her path.

"Damn!" he screamed as the other ship twisted away.

His golden rule for staying alive while flying was "never yield but always leave yourself an out." Folly had made him reckless, and he knew his reflexes were sluggish, but he was pissed at himself for letting this pilot provoke him.

Recovering his reason, he leveled off and threw down the skid flaps to reach a more reasonable speed. The jet took the torque and inertia strain, and the flashing red lights on his display turned yellow and then green.

Despite his irritation, he allowed himself a

faint smile when his AI read the Scorpion's registration: Lorelei Steward.

Good sense advised that he throttle back, but pride won out. Spotting the Scorpion silhouetted against a cloud, he jammed the throttle forward yet again.

Finally behind her, his smile broadened. She wouldn't slip away this time.

She pulled her jet into a violent oblique pop, rolled inverted until the nose pointed to the ground then returned to upright.

He stuck with her, move for move.

Abruptly she angled for the nearby mountain range. He chased her, low and fast, through a pass and down into a twisting canyon, rolling and pitching in a dizzying display of aerobatic skill. He kept close on her six until they blew out of the ravine.

In a desperate ploy to shake him, she turned back toward Melbourne's airspace and headed straight into a crowded flying highway.

Ryan was so close behind that it took a few seconds before he realized her blunder.

She had turned into an oncoming traffic lane.

The cockpit warning lights lit up the cabin as Ryan dodged a stream of oncoming vehicles. Up ahead, Lorelei ducked under a passenger liner that swerved directly into his path.

Time slowed to a crawl as he foresaw his fate—he could escape by pulling up—but that would force the crowded passenger liner to dive and crash into the ground.

"Damn it all!" he yelled and dove—leaving the liner a clear path to safety.

Through the neural interface, his AI shrieked,

TOO LOW! PULL UP!

TOO LOW! PULL UP!

He used every bit of expertise he could muster to twist, turn, and wrestle his jet into a controlled descent. His vision narrowed as the lights of city and ships gave way to a line of unyielding rocks zooming toward him. In a blink, he ran out of time—and altitude.

BRACE FOR IMPACT!

The Cobra plowed a trough a hundred meters long across the desert floor. Ryan sat in the cockpit, stunned and disoriented amid the flames and wreckage until his lungs convulsed from the dense smoke. An acidic stench and the taste of jet fuel assailed his nose and throat, rousing him from his stupor. Fumbling to unbuckle the safety harness, he held his breath until he could release the hatch and climb out of his ruined machine. Shaking hands searched his body for broken bones. To his relief, he was intact . . . if he didn't count the ringing in his ears and the blood that coursed down his face.

The maxim from flight school ran through his mind: "Any landing you walk away from . . ." But as he limped away, his beloved Cobra burned into a twisted mound of molten metal, its nose buried in the dusty red ground.

He shook his head at the wreck. "Captain Gallant is going to have my ass for this."

CHAPTER 2

Homecoming

The dark April thunderstorm that blanketed his shuttle-jet reflected Captain Henry Gallant's mood. The news from fleet headquarters was as disappointing as it was unexpected—a blow to both his ego and his career. Now he had to tell his wife and await her verdict.

They had married with their eyes open to the challenges of military life during wartime—frequent moves at the military's discretion, irregular periods of separation and worry, times of uncertainty, and difficult choices. Though they struggled at times, so far, they had managed to find a balance.

As he trudged up the steps to his one-bedroom apartment in the suburbs of Melbourne, he saw Alaina through the kitchen window. Her blonde hair pulled into a ponytail and the casual clothes in no way detracted from her natural grace and lithe beauty. He could already hear her singing while she fussed over the evening meal.

When he opened the door, the undeniable joy in her eyes lifted his mood. After three years of marriage, she was still as desirable as the day they wed.

"Henry, why didn't you tell me we're having guests for dinner?" Her playful pout only made her more beautiful.

"Guests?" he asked with a puzzled look.

"Don't tell me you've forgotten already! John called to ask what time he should get here."

"John Roberts is coming?"

"Yes. And I asked him to have Grace bring one of her special desserts."

"Grace too?"

"Of course," she replied, waving her hand as she turned back to the meal. Alaina's finger hovered over the entree selections and accompanying side dishes on the AI menu. "Steak okay? Or would you rather have lamb?"

Without waiting for his answer, she adjusted the oven settings for medium-well-done, lightly seasoned. The meal would be delivered to the dinner table at the pre-set time.

Gallant sighed at the thought of skimping on lunch for weeks to make up for the expense. Life in the capital city stretched even a captain's salary.

"Steak is fine, but I don't think John meant to bring Grace. I think he wanted a working evening with me, which you have now hijacked into a social event."

"I like John and Grace. Why shouldn't they

come and spend a pleasant evening with us?" asked Alaina in a huff.

"The *Warrior* returned from the Ross star system today. John is being debriefed at headquarters tomorrow."

"What does that have to do with you?"

"Remember the report on war strategy I wrote?"

"Of course. You drove me crazy for days, pacing the floor, and never once told me what it was about."

"John probably wants to give me a heads-up on his insights on the combat readiness of the Titans."

"Why couldn't he do that tomorrow?"

"The room will be filled with top brass, many who don't know him. He might want to ask for my advice."

"Why? Hasn't everyone already read your report?"

"That's the problem. Fleet command hated it," he said, his brows furrowing at the thought.

"They disagreed with you?"

"Disagreed is a modest assessment of the reaction. I stepped on some very big toes, and now it seems everyone at headquarters wants my head."

"Henry don't be silly. Who wouldn't value your expertise on Titan military strategy?" asked Alaina, squeezing his shoulder.

"Admiral Graves, for one."

"Why?"

"He sponsored an ambitious plan for a direct assault on a Titan star system. My report identified flaws in that strategy and advised against it. Now headquarters and Graves' staff are accusing me of everything from incompetence to treason."

"I can't believe that."

"Well, maybe not treason," admitted Gallant, "but my job is in serious jeopardy. They're even resurrecting that bugaboo about my lack of genetic engineering as a legitimate reason to doubt my judgment."

Alaina sighed. "Well, put that worry aside for this evening. John and Grace will be here within the hour. Let's enjoy a pleasant evening with friends. It'll do you good."

Gallant grumbled, "Let's not keep them too long. It's his first night back, you know."

Alaina started to protest, then her eyes widened. "Oh!" she said as the implication sank in.

When the doorbell rang, Alaina had a ready welcome.

"Hello, come in, come in. We're delighted to see you," she said, taking Grace's wrap and giving her a hug.

"Hello, Alaina. Henry," the couple said in unison.

Gallant wrapped his hand around Roberts'. "Good to see you home safely, John."

They held their grip for a long moment.

Roberts whispered, "I must speak to you about an urgent matter."

"Can it wait until after dinner?" asked Gallant, reading the impatience on Roberts' face.

He nodded with a grim expression. "After dinner then."

They arranged themselves comfortably in the living room.

Sitting in the chair across from John, Gallant brushed a lock of long brown hair off his brow. The youthful gesture had never left him.

Alaina asked, "How about a drink?"

"I'd love a martini," said Grace.

"Me too," said Roberts.

Alaina rose and dialed the AI for mixed drinks.

Grace said, "You have a charming apartment."

"Thank you," said Alaina. "Off-base housing is expensive, but I need to be near the university to continue my studies."

"Oh, that must be fulfilling," said Grace.

Gallant watched Grace as she sat next to her husband, holding his hand. Her joy and relief that he had returned home were palpable. Still, he noticed the tiny wrinkle lines around her eyes and wondered. An early mark of age, or perhaps worry?

It stood in contrast to Roberts' pronounced laugh lines that were an extension of his personality. He had filled out since the last time they'd seen each other. John had always been solidly built, but now he showed early signs of a potbelly.

He smiled and said, "I bear greetings from your old shipmates on the *Warrior*."

Gallant struggled to contain the emotions he knew showed on his face—jealousy, bitterness, frustration. To his mind, nothing was more pitiable than a sailor without a ship. But pride wouldn't let him acknowledge his failings.

Both men fell silent, letting the women talk.

Across from her guests, Alaina perched on the edge of the sofa with legs crossed and hands in her lap. Well accustomed to her husband's pensive moments, she carried the conversation by indulging in gossip. The conversation dissolved into random chitchat as they sipped their drinks until the AI chime announced dinner. Alaina glowed with pleasure as John and Grace piled compliments as high as the heaps of food on their plates.

During dinner, Gallant could hardly contain his impatience to talk shop with Roberts. He fidgeted and squirmed until Alaina glared at him.

Finally, to Gallant's relief, the plates were empty. The two men went into the living room while the women continued their conversation at the dinner table.

"Admiral Collingsworth is a remarkable man, but affairs are heating up. I hope he appreciates my concerns about the battle at Ross," said Roberts. "I've stuck my neck out with my assessment. I'm worried I'll get my head chopped off tomorrow."

"I wish I could do something to help. But I'm persona non grata at headquarters these days," said Gallant, frowning. "I'm afraid you face an uphill battle."

Roberts rubbed his chin. "The *Warrior's* mission was to collect and evaluate information and let headquarters' analysts fight over what it means. But my observations led me to critical conclusions that I felt compelled to state explicitly."

Gallant said, "I understand. My assignment on headquarters' strategic analysis team has put me in an awkward position. My interpretations are intensely unpopular and have even gotten me in trouble. You're walking into the same minefield. Some powerful men in the admiralty want to protect the good name of officers involved in that action. You need to be ready for an ambush."

"I'm a boat jockey, not a pencil pusher. I'm not interested in the political ploys of the capital. I need your help to get through this, Henry."

Gallant pressed his lips together. "What happened in the Ross system?"

Roberts rested his elbow on the armrest of the chair. His words were clipped and precise. "The *Warrior's* mission was to scout the star system before the assault, then to investigate some unusual findings on the outskirts of the system. I was as a distant observer to the aftermath of the battle."

Gallant nodded.

"The battle was the worst disaster in UP history. A complete failure of command and control."

Gallant was startled. "I knew it was bad, but I didn't imagine . . . ."

"To be fair, Admiral Butler had only old capital ships, none of the new construction. His battlecruisers had been stripped of most of their weapons and innards to make room for warp drives."

Gallant said, "We're in a technology race with the Titans to convert from interplanetary to interstellar ships. It hasn't been easy. In my report, I warned about mounting a major assault on a Titan system before the new construction ships were ready."

"Your concerns were borne out at Ross. I need your support in the debriefing tomorrow when I say that to their faces." He hesitated, looking at the hands clenched in his lap. "It's possible I'll face court-martial and removal from my command."

Gallant shook his head. "I won't be there. Even if I were willing to walk the plank with you, I don't have need-to-know authorization."

With a frown, he added, "Deliberately, I assume."

"I'll arrange access," said Roberts. "Don't let me down. Please."

Gallant's frown deepened.

Later, as he was leaving, Roberts looked Gallant in the eyes and pleaded, "Tomorrow?"

CHAPTER 3

The Gathering Storm

Overhead white puffs flecked the blue sky, and the sunlight shimmered on the glossy steel-and-glass fleet headquarters building. Seeing his distorted image reflected in the giant black monolith made Gallant reflect on his shortcomings and puzzle over his future. Setting his jaw, he pushed open the heavy doors. As he stepped inside, the embedded sensors scanned his ID pin.

The first person he saw at the security checkpoint was someone he knew only too well. Even at a single glance, Julie Anne McCall made a strong impression with her sharply pressed uniform, eye-catching figure, blonde hair, and seductive smile.

That smile was one of many professional contrivances the ruthless SIA agent used to mesmerize her opponents into revealing more than they should. At the sight of Gallant, it disappeared. "What are *you* doing here? You don't have clearance."

"My name was added at the last minute."

McCall glanced at the security guard, who confirmed with a nod, "Captain Gallant is on the access list."

Gallant saw her lips compress into a thin, disapproving line as he brushed past her.

The expansive amphitheater was usually reserved for important, large-scale debriefings of major mission reports. Gallant was surprised to find the auditorium echoing, the tiers of plush seats empty.

"Not here," McCall said, "in there," pointing to a door bereft of window or handle. She strode across and pressed her palm against the biometric scanner. The door slid open to reveal a smaller space with no other entrance.

The chamber had a whiteboard against one wall and a flat-panel video screen opposite. Many of the chairs in front were already occupied. Gallant recognized several officers, a few of whom were not a welcome sight, clustered together talking in low voices. Although the center of the room was brightly lit, the edges deepened into shadows. Indistinguishable figures moved about the perimeter, giving the room a menacing feel. The acoustics amplified the chatter but made words unintelligible.

McCall directed Gallant to a seat at the far corner of the room where she unexpectedly sat next to him. She inched her chair closer to his and whispered, "You are to speak to no one about your report without explicit authorization from me. It's been classified under black ops."

Bewildered, Gallant scowled.

She added, "We don't want you talking to the wrong people."

"Is that all?" he asked.

She shifted in her seat before answering. "Your information must get where it's needed."

Gallant frowned. "Don't you see the inherent contradiction in that?"

"That's why you need me—to make this work."

He forced a thin smile. "I'll try to suffer through and keep quiet."

Headquarters staff entered, and a few minutes later, Roberts arrived, taking a seat at the front table.

Gallant looked around the room to assess the strategic importance of the meeting. It was restricted to SIA and fleet analysts. Notably absent was Admiral Collingsworth. Gallant spent a few minutes considering what that might mean.

Perhaps he was called away on urgent matters.

Gallant watched as SIA agents situated themselves around the room. None spoke to him, but each one gave him a surreptitious glance.

He leaned over a few inches. "I thought this was going to be an informal presentation with a few reviewers—to hear Roberts' findings."

McCall ignored him.

Roberts stared straight ahead, lost in thought. He swallowed hard, and even from behind, Gallant could see the tension in his shoulders. At a nod from one of the guards, Roberts stood, gripping his tablet, and walked across the stage, each step echoing in the sudden silence. His face blanched as he cast a nervous gaze at the officers around him.

The door opened.

"AAAtennn... shun!" bellowed the guard.

Vice Admiral Graves, the Ross system theater commander, swept into the room with his staff and took the last seats at the head of the table. His long straight nose, broad chin, and bushy eyebrows gave him an appearance of shrewdness that his character lacked. His bulky frame made him appear as an imposing figure, but his ill-fitting uniform stretched over his puffy belly destroyed any similarity to a dignified posture. His twitchy jowls and red pitted skin dripped of sweat. Rather than looking like a commanding figure at ease, he appeared to be in discomfort.

"At ease," said an officer after the admiral took his seat.

Captain Agatha Turnbull, Graves' chief of staff, took her place at the podium. Waiting for the renewed babbling to die down, she adjusted her uniform and straightened her shoulders, then spent a full minute surveying the room in total silence. The dramatic pause had a solemnizing and somewhat forbidding effect.

Finally, she said, "Welcome to this debriefing of the action at the Ross star system. Over the next several hours, the SIA review team will question Captain Roberts and examine his data. Once we complete the preliminary information gathering, we'll open the floor to general questions." Her eyes scanned the room. "Now I'll turn the podium over to SIA representative Captain McCall."

The captain's smile was fleeting as she stood up and walked to the front of the room. "Captain Roberts is the commanding officer of the *Warrior*, a stealth recon ship stationed at the outer edge of the Ross system at the time of the battle. He collected extensive data and the black-box information from the destroyed ships. I'd like him to make an initial presentation of his findings."

Roberts stepped to the podium and said, "Thank you, Captain."

McCall continued smoothly, "But before he begins, I want to establish his background and experience." She asked several probing questions that seemed to Gallant to challenge Roberts' credibility. When she was satisfied, she nodded at the guard. On cue, several technicians swarmed in. One booted up the video feed, another connected the AI, and a third prepared to record the proceedings.

At another nod from McCall, Roberts took a coin-sized memory disc out of his pocket and inserted it into the podium's computer port. "The Ross action occurred nine light-years from Earth. This disc contains a reconstructed plot of the battle, along with the black-box audio and video feeds of the participating ships."

Roberts said, "Rear Admiral Butler was in command of the attack on the Ross star system. He had nine converted battlecruisers and eight destroyers to protect the landings. The first wave of the assault force faced little enemy opposition. The outermost planets, Able and Baker, had only small Titan forces building battle stations and communication satellites. A Marine battalion was assigned to attack each of them. The main Titan force of several thousand was building a spaceport over the third planet, Charlie. That was where the rest of the 2nd Marine Division landed."

He paused, dropping his gaze to the podium. "The initial phase was conspicuously successful."

An officer on Graves' staff muttered, "That sounds straight forward."

Roberts continued, "By the second day, the assault was well on its way to securing all the planets. The spaceport was captured, and a squadron of fighters was operational on Charlie."

He coughed and took a sip of water before continuing. "At this point, Admiral Butler decided to split his fleet into three divisions of three battlecruisers each. He stationed one division at each of the three planets, remaining with the third division at the main planet, Charlie. His stated intention was to prevent small Titan raiding parties from attacking the transports and landing sites."

Gallant thought, *dividing his forces invited trouble.*

"Further, he ordered most of the destroyers to the edge of the system as pickets to extend radar coverage."

"That doesn't seem unreasonable," commented McCall.

"In theory, it wasn't, but for some reason, their movements and locations weren't coordinated. In fact, due to their dispersion, the destroyers played no role in the subsequent action."

When Roberts hesitated, McCall prompted, "What happened next?"

Roberts' voice was strained but professional, like a doctor informing a patient of a deadly diagnosis. "A Titan fleet of nine battlecruisers and four destroyers dropped out of warp on the doorstep of the outermost planet. They attacked the first division before they even knew any enemy ships were in the star system. All three UP battlecruisers were annihilated. They didn't even have time to send a message warning the remaining divisions."

"How was that possible?" asked McCall.

Roberts' voice broke. "I can't believe the Titans planned it. It was damnable luck!"

"How?" repeated McCall.

"The Titans popped out of warp mere light-minutes from the first division, which was in orbit around planet Able. The stealth rating of the Titan cruisers and destroyers was '5' in comparison to the *Warrior's* '10.' But the light from the three orbiting battlecruisers was immediately visible to the Titans. It allowed them to calculate trajectories and launch missiles before detectable light rays from their ships reached the first division."

"A dangerous advantage," commented an officer on Graves' staff.

Roberts recovered his composure and resumed his professional tone. "Yes. Our battlecruisers were in such disarray at first that it took several minutes for them to start a defense. The first missiles struck before they had manned battle stations. No evasive action had begun. No antimissiles were launched. Shields were still in standby."

The audience was stunned. They stared in silence at the video screen, which all too graphically showed missiles intercepting the UP vessels.

"The initial missile bombardment was so devasting that all communications were destroyed. A continuous stream of targeting reports provided trajectories for more missiles. The Titans' follow-up salvos demolished what remained of the three battlecruisers."

The audience gave an audible groan as they watched the black-box video feeds from the battlecruisers and heard the cries of men and women caught in the destruction of their ships.

Gallant's hands gripped his knees as he watched the viewscreen. The plot now showed the enemy ships moving through the first division, leaving nothing but drifting debris and a handful of escape pods in their wake.

It was several distressing minutes later before the audience settled down enough for the presentation to continue.

Roberts said, "The second division was as unprepared as the first. It had received no warning message. At the time of the attack, they were blanketed by a solar flare. It distorted their sensors and added to the confusion. When the first contact report got through, they assumed it was the ships of the first division coming to join them. It wasn't until the Titans were within missile range that second division was able to penetrate the Titans' limited stealth technology and recognize the danger.

"And by then it was too late," said Roberts, wiping his brow. "Those lost moments proved fatal. Titan missiles were already on their way while the second division was still sounding battle stations. The *Achilles* managed to raise shields and deploy decoys, but they didn't have time for any maneuvers to avoid the missiles. After the first explosions, they tried to fire back, but they were already impaired."

Gallant watched the black-box video recordings from the bridge of the destroyed ships. The crew tried in vain to ward off the Titan missiles.

"The next ship in line was the *Ajax*. She turned to starboard and launched missiles, scoring a few hits on one enemy battlecruiser before she suffered fatal explosions. The last ship, the *Adroit*, turned to starboard to follow the *Ajax*. She too fired missiles and took evasive action and was not hit by the Titan's first barrage. But as the only remaining UP ship, she became the prime target of all nine Titan battlecruisers. She was overwhelmed minutes later."

Listening to the gripping black-box broadcast was heartbreaking. The audience understood the heroism it took for the crews to fight in the face of overwhelming odds.

Silence hung heavy in the room.

"Fortunately, the captain of the *Adroit* got a message out, alerting the third division of the enemy's presence."

Roberts shifted his weight from foot to foot as he continued, "Finally, the third division rallied the defenses of the third planet. The Marines sheltered in place, and the transports stopped unloading. Admiral Butler prepared the third division to meet the enemy."

McCall asked, "But the Titans turned away, correct? They didn't attack the third division or the Marines. Why?"

"I don't know. From what I can surmise from the videos and plot analysis, the Titans sustained only minor battle damage. Either they thought the alerted third division was more powerful than the others, or else they felt they had completed their mission. They left the system, ignoring the vulnerable transports and Marines."

The spectators sat in shock.

Roberts bit his lip and again wiped the sweat off his forehead. He took a deep breath and glanced at Gallant before adding, "Admiral Butler stated in his report that he drove the Titans off. After they left, he withdrew his remaining ships to Elysium. The Marines on Charlie were left to fend for themselves."

The hush in the room was broken by several staff officers muttering in angry voices. Roberts squirmed at the podium and cast pleading eyes toward Gallant.

Thinking of McCall's warning, Gallant hesitated before he set his jaw and stood up. He looked around the room and spoke with clarion clearness. "It's imperative we understand the causes of the failure at Ross."

The audience turned and focused on him. None of the faces looked pleased.

"We must acknowledge that the Titans have taken the technology lead."

Several heads shook, and Gallant felt the tension in the room rise.

"That's debatable," said one officer.

"It's incontrovertible. The Titans had superior sensory information. And they fired first and with a higher rate. The UP response was slow and poorly coordinated."

A few more voices rose in disagreement.

"They had an accurate assessment of the strategic situation that our leadership lacked," insisted Gallant.

Admiral Graves, visibly upset, demanded, "What exactly do you mean by lack of leadership?"

Gallant's eyes darkened to match his tousled hair, but he remained quiet for a portentous moment. He clenched his teeth and felt a bead of sweat on his brow. His chin jutting toward Graves defiantly, he said, "With all due respect, sir, Admiral Butler did not expect a major strike force to hit him, demonstrating a deficiency of vigilance. Further, he divided his command and misplaced his patrols."

All the blood drained from Graves' face, turning

it a pasty white. "How dare you cast blame in Admiral Butler's direction," he barked. His brow darkened, and his voice rose as he struggled to maintain his composure. "He acted on the best information available."

Gallant took a deep breath. "Admiral Butler's preparations were based on what he believed the enemy *would* do rather than what they *could* do. And what the enemy could do was to strike fast and hard."

"Unfounded speculation," said one officer, rising with a scowl.

"That's slander," another growled.

"Disrespecting a senior officer!" said another.

Gallant couldn't stop himself. "Butler left the Marines without any support. A relief effort must be undertaken as soon as possible."

"That's your opinion," said Graves, his voice clipped and filled with resentment. "The Marines are in a strong position with adequate supplies. They can defend themselves against enemy action."

Gallant said, "Still, it would be wise to make provision for relief." After a moment, he added, "Sir."

"I've received assurances from Admiral Butler that the Marines are sufficiently protected for now."

"Yes, sir, but the Titans *could* strike again to finish what they started."

"There is time to deal with that when needed," said Graves with finality, and turned his back on Gallant.

Gallant knew it was hopeless to argue with a man who was more concerned with his reputation than with military necessities. Graves had clearly made up his mind, and on the face of it had a reasonable argument.

Graves' frown deepened as he glared at Roberts. "What would *you* attribute the losses to?"

Roberts hesitated only briefly. "Admiral Butler's lack of information about the Titan deployment and intentions led him into mispositioning his fleet. The fact that his ships were old hybrid battlecruisers made them vulnerable to the newer, more powerful class of Titan ships. The combination of Titan stealth technology and human failures in identifying and communicating the attack were also major contributors."

"Anything else you wish to add?" asked McCall.

"Yes."

"What more could you possibly have to say?" demanded Graves.

"More but different, sir," said Roberts, taking out a second disc. We found alien artifacts of another alien species. With evidence that indicates they could also be fighting the Titans."

"Go on."

"At the far outer reaches of the Ross system, we found alien satellite space stations and drones, all of which had been damaged or destroyed in battle. My techs were able to discern that the weapons that destroyed some of them were Titan. Yet, the satellite remains were of a technology we have never seen before. Also, we found remnants of Titan warships nearby, suggesting that a battle had occurred between the two species."

With a look at McCall, Roberts concluded, "I have a treasure trove of data and physical evidence that should keep SIA happy for a long time."

As the meeting broke up, McCall pulled Gallant aside. "You don't have to make yourself a lightning rod every time? Do you?"

She considered him for a moment before adding, "Wait here."

After twenty minutes, she returned and said, "You've been relieved of duty with the fleet headquarters' strategic analysis office."

"I thought as much," said Gallant with a scowl. He stood silently for a minute to get a grip on his emotions.

"I have new orders for you."

"What if I'm not ready to take on a new assignment?"

"This is not a request. You are a military officer."

"When and where?" asked Gallant sullenly.

"Everything you need is in this file. You report tomorrow at 0800."

Gallant said nothing.

"Disappointed?" she asked, just a hint of a smile on her lips.

"I follow orders. As always."

"You don't sound happy. You should take that up with the admiral."

CHAPTER 4

Top Gun

At over one hundred square km, the Melbourne spaceport was Earth's largest space shipyard. From its geosynchronous orbit, the shipyard could launch and recover vehicles. The dome terminal and hangar facilities supported space tugs that assisted large spaceships. Several fighter squadrons operated out of the spaceport, including those in training at Top Gun Academy.

"Attention on deck!" bellowed a student as Gallant entered the classroom at the academy.

The young men and women rose as one and stood at attention.

He relaxed as he surveyed the fresh faces.

"At ease."

The class of junior officers took their seats. They eyeballed him as he strolled through the room. When he reached the instructor's platform, he said, "You were chosen as Top Gun candidates because of your outstanding performance. Once you leave here, you will assume leadership positions in the new generation of spacecraft carriers."

Gallant took a moment to stare at the enthusiastic faces. As he remembered his experiences as a midshipman, he fought down a flood of regrets. He wondered if these pilots would benefit from his expertise or come to regret his mentoring.

He said, "You're all exceptional, but you'll find my standards are exceptionally high. You'll be challenged as never before. A handful of you will become Top Gun finalists. And only one will graduate with that title. I promise you; it's a goal worth striving for."

Gallant could already guess who the top leaders would be and who wouldn't make it. He recognized several faces. He focused his gaze on Ensign Ryan, whom he had mentored in several training exercises.

BANG!

The door slammed open, showing a stunning redhead silhouetted in the door frame. Every head turned her way.

She said, "I apologize for being late, sir. I was detained by security."

"Detained?"

She stammered, "There was a . . . hold . . . on my clearance. Traffic violation, sir. I have to report back after class."

"Take a seat, Ensign Steward," said Gallant with a frown. "I will not tolerate the deliberate disregard of safety regulations. Taking a risk in combat is necessary, but carelessness due to a false sense of invulnerability can be extremely dangerous."

Gallant explored their faces before continuing, "The judgment to distinguish a calculated risk from a reckless gamble is what makes a great pilot. Show poor judgment, and I'll dismiss you. Prove yourself a righteous risktaker, and you'll advance."

He stole a glance at Ryan as Lorelei found a seat at the back of the room.

Ryan slumped in his chair and cast his gaze to the floor to avoid eye contact with her, but a flash of guilty recognition crossed her face.

For a few seconds, Gallant struggled with the mental calculus of how to handle these two, then he shoved the thought away and focused on the class in front of him.

He said, "I'd like to get to know a little about each of you."

This surprised the students. They were used to impersonal teachers who delivered stern lectures.

"My call sign is 'Natural'," said Gallant. "I wasn't genetically engineered. I lost my parents at an early age and was raised by my grandmother until I went to the academy. My natural abilities have let me contribute to the struggle against the Titan."

The students exchanged glances. Many had already heard a great deal about their teacher's unusual characteristics.

Gallant asked each student to speak for a minute describing their background.

Lorelei said, "My home is on this continent. When I was a child, I loved climbing trees. My brother

H. Peter Alesso

would yell at me, 'not too high, not too high.' James is now a Marine on some distant planet. I pray for him every night."

She took a deep breath before continuing, "I'm still trying to climb high—only now it's to the stars."

There was light laughter.

Gallant smiled. "Your call sign is 'Flame'."

Someone in the back hollered, "As in flame-out?"

"No," said Gallant. "Not flameout, Mister Ryan, but your call sign will be 'Lucky'. As in, you'll be lucky if your number of landings equals your number of take-offs."

There was considerable laughter peppered with several hoots.

When his turn came, Ryan revealed that his parents died in an accident while he was a teenager and he moved between foster families until he claimed the navy as home.

He added, "I'm going to be Top Gun!"

Gallant said, "We'll see about that."

Then he turned to a huge huggable pilot, Ensign Joe Flannery, and said, "Your callsign will be 'Bear.'"

As he continued around the room. He named Samuel Rhodes, 'Dusty,' and Edward Decatur, 'Hot-shot.'

Even if he hadn't been wearing an AI earbud, Gallant could've guessed what his students were thinking.

What's next?

After several weeks of flight school, the ensigns were bored with lectures and endless simulations. They were ready for mock combat exercises and bending on some serious speed.

Early in the morning, the class gathered in the flight hangar's Ready Room at Melbourne's spaceport for a final briefing.

Gallant said, "You will be flying Viper fighters for this exercise. They're equipped with the latest high-tech elements that you'll find when you're deployed."

Ryan smiled the moment he laid eyes on the F-789 Viper I. It was a sleek, elegant starfighter capable of accelerating to 0.3 C in less than six hours. It had missiles and a pulsed laser cannon capable of punching through titanium armor.

Gallant said, "This fighter can operate in the stormy upper atmosphere of Jupiter as well as the vacuum of outer space. Its gimbal spin gyro generates enough torque to flip the ship end-over-end in a matter of seconds. But remember that while the engine is powerful enough to change speed and direction rapidly, it can't work miracles."

The class had already covered how the physics of space combat differed from air combat. In space, an enemy could theoretically approach from any direction. But spaceships were limited by orbital dynamics—not just their own ship's orbit around a planet, but that planet's orbit around the sun.

He said, "Your AI neural interface is an essential tool. It features deep-learning and comprehensive knowledge. Listen to its recommendations but remember that it isn't an intelligent being, so don't treat it as such. You are the creative intelligence in combat. The neural interface can only inform and enhance your decision making."

The mock combat was scheduled to take place above Venus's stormy weather with a hard floor of one hundred kilometers.

Gallant said, "Remember, that while there are no rules in combat, there are rules during training. You will observe the 'hard deck' and engine limitations during this exercise."

He said, "I will take three students at a time. Lucky, you'll be Flame's wingman flying the Viper I for Blue Flight. Blue Flight will fly Combat Space Patrol (CSP) for a satellite which we'll designate as the mock spacecraft carrier, *Orion*."

"Bear, you're with me. We'll be Red Flight—bandits in the Viper II. We'll target *Orion*."

The Viper II fighter-bomber was essentially a Viper I fighter with an externally mounted heavy missile rack that could be ejected during a dogfight.

The pilots looked at him, eager to begin.

"Man your ships," said Gallant.

"OK. Fights on," said Ryan, sprinting to his ship. "I feel the need for speed."

He glanced at Lorelei who went through her preflight checks, hardly acknowledging him.

The Viper fighters taxied to their starting positions and prepared to launch.

The pilots put on their neural interface headsets.

Wearing the neural interface headsets, the pilots *felt* an expanded awareness of the world as they visualized the ship controls and equipment. Dozens of silicon probes touched their skin at key points, reading and translating brain-wave patterns directly into flight commands. Pilots moved the ship merely by thinking about direction and speed. With the enhanced speed and accuracy of thought-control, the manual stick was functional but used primarily as a backup.

Even after years of use, the interface remained a challenge for Gallant. As a Natural, he had to concentrate his mental effort.

The Vipers scrambled, each one blasting a wave of exhaust across the runway. Once aloft, they managed to stay in formation until they moved beyond the standard Earth orbit.

The Blue Flight accelerated to 0.1C and covered the hundred million kilometers to reach Venus in a few hours. When they reached the *Orion,* they took up their assigned patrol stations and waited for the Red Flight to appear.

The Red Flight was not far behind with Flannery flying as Gallant's wingman.

Gallant's first command was to accelerate to the far side of Venus. Then he flipped around on his gyros and decelerated, skimming the top of the soupy atmosphere to remain hidden until the hull glowed bright red. As the Viper pierced the stratosphere, the hull creaked and unveiled various external noises—a change from the silence of deep space. The ship developed a slight but noticeable vibration.

The tiny Viper reminded Gallant of ships he had piloted before. Each had a painful memory attached, but he quickly dispelled his momentary sense of loss. Instead, he focused on the mission. He let Venus fill the viewscreen. The imagery stimulated his imagination as well as his awareness. He was beginning to enjoy the exercise.

Bank to port.

He performed a wingover as the ship shifted in orbit. The maneuver caused the planet to swirl around in his viewport, adding a visual spectacle to the audible noises.

Accelerate.

The thunderous nuclear engines thrust the craft forward. It emerged from the atmosphere with the sun shining off its polished hull as Gallant climbed to a higher altitude over Venus.

The mock combat had begun.

Ryan called over tac1, "Flame, bandits spotted ten light-seconds out 030 up10. High and fast, on a heading toward *Orion*."

Lorelei said, "They're making a straight shot at the 'carrier.' We'll intercept at .1C in thirty seconds."

Gallant gazed through the Viper's canopy at *Orion* in the distance.

His AI reported, "Viper emissions detected."

The location and flight characteristics flashed into Gallant's mind.

The Blue Flight was coming head-on placing him squarely in the danger zone. Over the intercom, Flannery reported, "Blue Flight is banking hard to starboard."

Gallant changed the Red Flight's course and dove at the enemy combatants. He said, "Concentrate your fire on the lead Viper. I'll target high. You take low."

He thought, *Select missiles.* The AI activated the mock missiles for launch. The ready button flashed on his dashboard.

Flannery mimicked Gallant's maneuvers. The two of them swung into position.

"Six seconds to intercept," said Gallant over tac2.

"You got it."

"Bear, come further toward the target."

"Watch it, Natural. These guys are really moving!" Flannery warned.

Gallant banked to a new heading.

"The second has gone silent. I've lost trace."

Gallant said, "Never mind him. I'm lined up on the leader and ready to fire. Sync with me."

Flannery said, "On target. Missiles locked on."

"Fire missiles."

"Missiles are hot."

A moment later, Flannery reported, "No joy. Signals jammed."

Gallant willed Blue Flight to come back into

range, but Flannery said, "Targets have changed course."

"Jettison external missile rack. Hard to starboard," ordered Gallant.

Without the burden of external racks, the Viper IIs were now able to fight their opponents on equal terms.

Gallant observed the ship handling abilities of the pilots as they maneuvered. Flannery was a hair slower and a smidgen less accurate than Ryan.

The display heading spun as Gallant swung his ship to an intercept course and began a new attack run.

The two flights blew past each other and turned for another pass.

"Hell! They're coming around too fast. Abort! Abort!" shouted Gallant.

He thought, *hard to port!* But the Blue Flight had already opened fire on Flannery and launched simulated missiles.

The radar spiked with incoming missiles. Gallant ordered, "Release countermeasures. Start jamming."

"Aye aye."

Blue Flight scored simulated missile hits on Flannery. The AI designated his fighter disabled. He limped out of range.

Ryan whooped over tac 1, "Splash one!"

With Flannery out of commission, Gallant headed for *Orion* alone. Coming around again, Blue Flight ganged up on him.

He dove toward the edge of the atmosphere to escape.

The proximity alert sounded. The AI screamed...

TOO LOW! PULL UP!

TOO LOW! PULL UP!

Gallant's Viper skimmed the upper atmosphere and glowed bright red from the spiking hull temperature. He was dangerously close to the hard deck limit.

As soon as Blue Flight dove to follow him, Gallant hit max thrusters and executed a tight loop followed by a wing-over. He twisted and wrestled the machine until its torque and inertia dampening gyros squealed. He was pressed so hard into his seat he couldn't draw a breath, but his maneuver fooled them.

Gallant was now behind the Blue Flight.

Ryan maneuvered wildly to avoid being targeted, but an instant later, Gallant squeezed his yoke trigger and yelled, "Guns. Guns."

Red laser pulses flashed—the AI scored hits on Ryan's fighter—he was toast.

Lorelei threw the stick over and tried to fire back, but she was too late.

Gallant scored a damaging hit which caused her to turn away.

His next maneuver fooled Lorelei into moving too far from *Orion*, leaving him an uninterrupted path to the target, which he took.

A few minutes later, the AI reported, "Red Flight has scored the winning hits."

Later that day, they met for a debriefing in the Melbourne hanger.

Lorelei wore a sheepish grin as if she were caught shoplifting.

She whispered, "Sorry."

"Forget it, we both messed up," said Ryan.

"Sit," said Gallant. He reconstructed the scenario and showed the early situation. When he described the final combat sequence, he said, "This is where it all went wrong. What were you thinking at this point?"

They remained quiet.

"Ryan, you left your wingman position, and your reckless tactics made you vulnerable."

Ryan sheepishly cast his gaze to the floor and remained mute.

"Lorelei, the Viper sensor suite is optimized to minimize relativistic distortion in the forward direction. This gives you the most accurate data on objects directly in front of you. But there are blind spots abaft the beam to the port and starboard."

Moving a step closer to Lorelei, he leaned forward and whispered, "I maneuvered into your blind spot and suckered you into moving out of position."

Her face was awash with embarrassment and frustration. But she had a quick wit and did not allow the situation to rob her of her sense. She said, "It was my fault. I was lined up to shoot but couldn't get a missile lock. Then I lost track of you. I should have maintained security on *Orion*, but I swung around to keep searching for you."

Gallant said, "You both lost situational awareness. Lucky, you should've remained as wingman to cover Flame's blind spots. And Flame, you should have kept to your mission of protecting *Orion*. In combat, that'll cost you not only your partner's life but your own, as well."

He let them stew for a minute before continuing, "Before you're through here, you will absorb everything about the weapon and flight characteristics of the enemy's systems. You must recognize their tactics as well as your own."

He smiled, "You will gather this information in painful doses."

They flinched.

He said, "I was impressed with your flying, but I was unimpressed with your combat choices. You wanted to shoot when you should have been playing defense. You don't always get a kill shot. Sometimes it's smart to break off and fight another day."

CHAPTER 5

A Simple Request

"Politics has crept into military decision making," said Admiral Collingsworth with a grimace.

"Politics?" asked Gallant.

"Butler should never have led the Ross mission. For that matter, the Ross mission was premature. We should have waited until the new construction ships were ready—as you recommended."

"I'm glad my report reached you even if headquarters didn't heed it."

"The presidential campaign is in full swing now. Kent's main opponent is Gerome Neumann."

"I don't see ..."

"Butler is Graves' man, and Graves is Neumann's. Neumann has made the aggressive prosecution of the war the focus of his campaign," said Collingsworth. Dropping his voice, he added, "That and the genetic engineering issue."

He turned his perpetually world-weary eyes on Gallant before switching his gaze to the lopsided stack of documents on his desk.

"Now why have you come here and interrupted me in the middle of my day?" asked the admiral, the corners of his mouth drawn down.

"Sir, I request reassignment to fleet duties," said Gallant.

"Why?"

"Sir, the defeat at Ross has left the Marines vulnerable. After Captain Roberts' presentation, I assume a relief force is being mounted. I want to be a part of it."

He rose and fixed his penetrating gaze on Gallant. Even drawing up to his full height with a ramrod-straight posture, Gallant towered over him. That didn't faze the admiral.

Collingsworth had a reputation as a ferocious commander in battle, but he was also known for his measured temperament when dealing with his men. Now he stepped around the desk, thrusting his face forward until Gallant could feel the anger simmering under his polished demeanor. The admiral's eyes blazed, his brows lowered, and his cheeks reddened.

He said, "The war is running hot. The Titans are still killing our people and destroying our ships. Do you suppose that I don't want to join the men I send into the heat of battle? That I wouldn't welcome the chance to fight alongside my shipmates, risking what they risk?"

His voice rising, the admiral added, "Do you think I like staff work in the backwater of this damnable war any more than you do?"

Gallant stood rigid, feeling the man's zeal. "Sir, you chased the last of the Titan ships out of the Solar System, and the president chose you to command the Home Fleet to safeguard Earth."

The admiral took several deep breaths. "I'm 107 years old, but I still have fire in my veins. I want to go to the aid of those Marines as much as you do. Do you think I wouldn't turn my command over in a minute if the president would let me?"

Gallant moved his lips but said nothing.

Collingsworth sat down and sighed, "What's behind your request?"

"I've been on shore duty for several years now. Any number of expert pilots can perform my duties as head of the Top Gun school. And my report on Titan readiness for Fleet Strategic Analysis is complete. I feel I could better serve if I'm deployed with the fleet. Especially now, after the fiasco at Ross."

"That report of yours overstepped the mark. You ignored the chain of command and crossed the line with your sweeping strategic recommendations. And you've put the entire admiralty under scrutiny with your criticism of Admiral Butler. Now you have the audacity to ask to walk away from all that and leave me to clean up your mess?"

Gallant dropped his eyes to the floor. "I withdraw my request, sir."

"Damn right you do! You're on staff here because you have unique abilities. Abilities that we need to fight this war, or I'd shoot you myself for that idiotic request."

The old man leaned back and sank deeper into his chair. He sighed, "You're part of a team. If you don't grasp that simple fact, then you're no use to me. I will use you where I deem you add the most value to my team of military professionals."

"I understand, sir. I apologize."

"Good. Trust me; you'll get your chance. I need your skillset. I do need you on the frontline. But it will happen when I determine the time is right," said Collingsworth with finality.

He picked up a document from his desk and added, "Despite Admiral Graves' strident objections, I've passed your report, *Combat Readiness of the Titans*, up the chain of command."

In a hushed voice, he added with an appraising look, "The president wants to meet you. Captain McCall will make the arrangements. That's all. Dismissed."

CHAPTER 6

Let Some Dreams Go

Alaina opened her eyes to the sound of typical early-morning activity outside the apartment. Gallant was already sitting on the edge of the bed beside her. He gazed out the open window as a cool breeze blew the fragrant scent of spring into the room.

"Did the traffic wake you?" asked Alaina. "Have you been up long?"

"A while," he said, staring at the morning's red sky. There was only a glimmer of light through the curtains.

"Is something troubling you?"

"No," he shook his head, "nothing important."

Alaina was a good listener and a better psychologist than most wives. She was an expert at distinguishing between his daydreams and deliberation. And she also recognized when he downplayed legitimate worry.

She sat up next to him and leaned over to kiss his cheek, deliberately letting her dressing gown slip from her shoulder to expose her breasts. He turned and reached for her, but she drew back from his caress.

"Is it safe?"

"Is what safe?" he asked in surprise.

"Traveling between stars."

"You're joking, right?"

"No. I want to know."

"Right now?"

"Why not?"

"Well, in the first place that isn't a topic I usually discuss with a naked woman in my bed. And in the second place, you've never asked about it before, in all our years together."

She persisted, "Tell me. It's important to me."

Gallant snickered, "It's safer than flying a Cobra jet over Melbourne."

"Oh?"

"Did that help?"

She shook her head, wistfully. "Not really."

He grunted.

Lost in thought, she mused, "When I was a little girl, I wanted to know lots of stuff. I had great hopes and dreams."

"Such as?"

"I wanted to be a princess," she giggled. "And I wanted to fly and . . . and I wanted to be a superwoman."

"You *are* a superwoman," said Gallant, kissing her lips tenderly.

"Thank you, Dear," she sighed. "But when I grew up, I had to let some dreams go. Now, I'd just like to be a good person in an imperfect world."

"Don't let that one go."

She smiled and changed the subject. "What is it that *you* want?"

He said nothing, but Aliana knew he was thinking.

A ship.

She stroked his bare arm. "Are you enjoying the academy?"

"I like Rob Ryan. He's courageous and dedicated to the fleet, but he can be reckless and immature. Lorelei Steward is equally talented and has great flying skills, despite being far too impulsive. They could be capable leaders, but they've got a lot to learn. I'm afraid they may not live long enough to develop the discipline they need."

Shivering as the wind picked up, she chafed her arms. "Brrr, it isn't as warm as I thought."

He let his lips trail down the gooseflesh on her arm before strutting half-naked to the window.

Admiring his sculptured physique as he pulled the pane down, she stepped behind him and traced a finger down the scar that ran from his left shoulder down his back.

"You've accumulated a lot of souvenirs over the years."

"Yeah, I have," he smirked.

She drew him back to the bed and patted the spot beside her, inviting him closer.

The look she gave him spoke more than any romantic words—it was a look of lovers rediscovering each other.

He leaned in and wrapped his arms around her, feeling the rising intimacy at her soft touch. Her body melded to his, warm and inviting, as they kissed. An electric tingle ran through his body, and she responded with equal fervor, as they explored, aroused, and finally satisfied their mutual passion.

Afterward, with Alaina naked and still wrapped in his arms, he asked, "Are you still cold?"

"No," she said, but snuggled closer, and he pulled the blanket over them both.

CHAPTER 7

The Enemy of My Friend

April continued to be a stormy month as low dark clouds threatened more showers. Gallant climbed into the shuttle-jet next to McCall and slammed the hatch shut.

"Strap in," she said. "We'll be at the president's country home in twenty minutes."

A few minutes later, the jet skimmed over the stark landscape. Gallant took in the panoramic view, enthralled by the contrasts between stark desert, craggy mountains, and bustling cities. He dreaded the thought of war assaulting this rugged yet beautiful land.

He tugged at his uniform jacket, wishing he'd had time to spruce up. But before he knew it, he was being ushered into the outer chamber of the president's private office.

A rugged-faced Marine stood at rigid attention outside a luxury suite. Its opulent carpet, vaulted ceilings, and antique furnishings were reserved for receiving dignitaries.

A side door opened, and Captain George Gregory appeared.

"Red!" said Gallant.

Gallant's old friend was a redheaded giant with a bodybuilder torso, an agreeable brow, and a mischievous grin. His rich, baritone voice filled the air. "Henry. It's wonderful to see you. How're you? How's married life treating you?"

"I'm great and so is Alaina. How've you been? Still a carefree bachelor?"

They might have spent a couple of minutes gossiping on recent promotions and assignments if McCall hadn't urged them onward. Still, they managed a few excited comments about Kelsey Mitchel before Red received a signal.

Reluctantly, Red led Gallant into the president's office, leaving McCall in the luxurious outer room.

At first glance, the private sanctum of the great leader reminded him of Red's family home. The space was crammed with intimate personal possessions of President Richard G. Kent, collected over a lifetime. Memorabilia, trinkets, and photos of his wife and family crowded on the shelves. Drawings by his grandchildren hung over a display case of family trophies, ribbons, and awards.

"Come in, come in, Henry," boomed the commanding voice of the president as he waved Gallant to a chair across from his sofa. The man's youthful face and physique, the product of Earth's finest genetic engineering, belied his advanced years.

He wrapped his hands around Gallant's hand, pumping it like an affectionate grandfather. "Glad to meet you at last. Have a seat. I've followed your exploits with growing fascination. I said to Teddy many years ago, 'that boy bears watching.'"

"I . . . I, huh," fumbled Gallant taken aback by the nature of the president's boisterous welcome.

'Teddy' was Theodore Gilbert, the secretary of defense who occupied the nearby chair. He showed his winning smile as he observed the younger man's reactions.

"How about joining me in a midday snack?" asked the leader of the United Planets as he tore his sandwich in half. "It's grilled cheese and ham. My favorite."

"Thank you, Mr. President." Gallant took the sandwich and placed it on a plate in front of him.

"Sorry to ask you to drop by so abruptly, but I never seemed to have a minute to myself anymore. When my afternoon appointment was unavoidably delayed, I grabbed the opportunity." Kent took a large swallow of coffee and said, "Ahh, no one makes coffee like my Maria. She prides herself in brewing it special for me."

Gallant blinked as he recalled that Maria was the president's wife of sixty-six years.

"Here. Have a cup," Kent said pouring some of the steaming hot brew into a cup and shoving it across the table.

"Excellent," said Gallant taking a couple of sips.

"Teddy, the reports I've read on this fellow, not to mention the ones he's written, have given me goosebumps over the years. What do you think of him?"

"I think we need to keep an eye on this young man, Mr. President."

The pair shared a laugh.

Gallant watched and wondered where this interview was leading.

Then Kent's face sobered, and he gave a meaningful look at Captain Gregory, who nodded and promptly left the room. The president sipped at his coffee again and said, "They're a hard people to make out, those Titans. You made a reconnaissance mission to their home-world. What're the Titans really like, Henry?"

Gallant hesitated, debating how to reply to such a multifaceted question.

"They're highly intelligent, an autistic trait cultivated by genetic engineering."

Kent nodded, encouraging him to expand on the thought.

"Several hundred years ago, the Titans had a tiny autistic savant population. When they started genetic engineering, they followed an approach like ours, eliminating disease and altering physical characteristics. It was when they began experimenting with species-wide improvements, rather than individual characteristics, that they got into trouble. After a series of wars, a dictator emerged. An autistic savant, he mandated that all embryos be altered using his genetic material. It was several years before the public realized that millions of autistic savants were being born."

Gallant continued, "As a species, the Titans lack both empathy and sympathy. Their language is complex, a labyrinth of strict grammar and convoluted syntax, but resonating with melodious sounds. Their teachings are rife with contradictory concepts. At the same time, after so many generations of restrictive governance, their language cannot express ideas such as liberty and individual creativity. Their communication network stimulates thought but only insofar as it reinforces desired behavior. Their society is dedicated to expanding their empire. And they're working at lightning speed to match our warp drive and stealth technologies."

The older men nodded, and Kent leaned forward intently.

"You sound as if any political compromise with the Titans is impossible."

Gallant hesitated. "Not impossible, Mr. President but unlikely given their history and character."

Teddy said, "The only option is to beat them, as we already did here in the Solar System. Then we must pursue them to their home planet to drive the point home."

The president said, "Technology is changing at a breakneck pace. We're in a transition period, much like the navy of the American Civil War. At that time, many of their ships were still under sail but were being converted to steam with armor plating. They were neither fish nor fowl."

Teddy said, "Yes, Mr. President. But today new ships—dreadnaughts and spacecraft carriers— are being built from scratch as fast as our yards will allow."

"But who knows when any of them will be ready?" wondered the president. "I need your assessment, Henry, of how much time do we have before they catch up."

Gallant described the Titan's emphasis on their strict code of obedience, outlining a possible production schedule that would lead to privation for the Titan people. Kent grunted in appreciation from time to time and listened with only occasional interjections.

Finally, the president said, "I must decide if we are to play offense or defense. It's a puzzle. If I'm aggressive and send too much of our fleet to fight lightyears away, we might be vulnerable at home. But if I remain passive, stick close to home, the Titans could build up an overwhelming force. Even with the intelligence you've gleaned, it's hard to know. Most of the briefings I get are more bewildering than helpful. Tell me young man, what's your view?"

Teddy interjected, "In your report, you advised against sending Admiral Graves' fleet on a direct assault on Titan star systems. Why?"

Gallant pondered a moment before choosing a historical analogy. "Our strategy must follow the path of England when it faced the French in the nineteenth century."

"England?"

"Yes, Mr. President. Consider the similarity of the vast oceans of Earth to the expanse of space. The isolated islands of the British Empire were as remote to them as distant star systems are to us."

"Humph. Interesting."

"At the time, England had the greatest navy on Earth, but the French had the greatest army and threatened to invade the island."

"I recall."

"England won the decisive battle of Trafalgar, but it was a near run thing. Demonstrating the importance of maintaining a dominant home fleet."

"Thank you for the parallel, Henry. It's the most cogent image of the situation I've received. I keep telling Admiral Collingsworth we must keep him at home to protect us, as you say."

"Oh, we'll do that, Mr. President, don't worry," interjected Teddy.

"Gallant, consider yourself at my beck and call. I want you to be available whenever I need an interpretation of Titan activity or a fresh perspective on strategic thinking. I'm sick and tired of getting watered-down tidbits when what I need is actionable intelligence and cogent ideas. Teddy, give Henry your direct access code so he can pass on hot information or deductions without going through that swamp they call channels."

The secretary nodded.

"Henry, you're a unique officer. I want to use

you to our best advantage. I'm confident in your discretion in what you forward to me."

"Thank you, Mr. President."

Teddy dropped a heavy hand on Gallant's arm and said, "You may think that becoming a confidant of the president is a good thing for your career. But be aware that in acquiring the president's ear . . . you're also acquiring the president's enemies."

Gallant opened his mouth, but before he could speak Kent gave a dry laugh. "After a lifetime as a politician, I've managed to make more than a few enemies. Gerome Neumann is just the latest. And given your disfavor with both him and Admiral Graves, you're probably the only man in Melbourne more despised than me."

The president chuckled at his own cleverness. The secretary of defense rocked back and forth with mirth.

Just as quickly, the laughs faded. "One more thing before you go. You also have a reputation as an ace fighter pilot. I want your opinion on the new spacecraft carriers. Will they be effective against the Titans?"

"Absolutely, Mr. President. We should launch a series of hit-and-run attacks on the enemy's outlying star systems. Enough of them to keep the Titans wondering where we'll strike next."

The president nodded. "I'm afraid this is going to be a long war. I'm grateful for men and women like you. Your expertise gives me confidence that we will prevail. Thank you for your service."

CHAPTER 8

Liftoff

L *iftoff's* décor featured salvaged fighter parts including a canopy, a wingtip, and an AI component. Signed historic photos plastered the wall behind the bar. Tonight, the officer's club pulsed with laughter and loud music. Bodies crammed both the bar and the dance floor, celebrating the return of a squadron from deployment.

Henry Gallant was standing in the center of the club when he saw a face—a body—that hit him like a laser blast. He had often imagined meeting Kelsey Mitchel again, envisioned sharing the pleasure of her company. But these fantasies always faded into a vague mist . . . until now. As she approached, he swallowed hard and felt his hands go clammy.

She walked in solo which was kind of alluring by itself. Her mouth turned up, and her eyes lit with delight as she moved effortlessly through the crowd toward him.

So intent was he on her approach that he didn't quite hear her greeting.

"I said, 'hello.' It's good to see you, Henry."

A confusing cascade of emotions washed over him—joy, passion, guilt—in such quick succession that the rush left him feeling drained.

"Hello, Kelsey," he stumbled. "The past seems to have a way of catching up with us."

"It's been a long time."

"A lifetime."

"I've missed you," she whispered, leaning closer.

He thought he saw something in her eyes, a flicker of shared memories. "You're lovely, as always."

"Am I?" she asked mockingly.

His color rose under her unabashed stare.

"Yes. But . . . different."

"Different how?" she asked, crinkling her brow.

"Different from . . . what I had expected, I guess."

"So? Have I changed so much?"

"That's not what I meant."

"What did you mean? Why are you so mysterious? It only piques my curiosity."

He shrugged and threw up his hands. "I don't know why I find emotions so hard to express."

His eyes searched her face for a long moment. Then he abruptly changed the subject. "You're a recon pilot now?"

Kelsey nodded. "My commission was reinstated. I'm with the 10th Recon Squadron, assigned to a new construction carrier, the *Constellation*."

"What about your medical discharge?"

"I volunteered," she explained. "It's amazing what desperate recruiters will do these days to meet their quota. I'm wasn't quite good enough for fighters, but fine for recon. And now the new stealth technology has made recon missions more important than ever."

"I'm glad. You always had a passion for flying. Is Gerome Neumann alright with that?"

"I avoid my father-in-law now that he has announced his candidacy for president. He's none-too-pleased with the wife of his heroic son refusing to be part of the rich family's parade."

"Heroic son?"

"Yes, he was decorated. The official version of Anton's death said nothing of his dispute with you or of McCall's actions. It was hushed up to protect Neumann's chances for political office. I'm fine with that, and I'm guessing you and McCall aren't disputing those findings."

"All that wealth and power?" asked Gallant. "That's a lot to walk away from."

"Not so much, depending on what you consider worthwhile." She shrugged. "I'll admit, it took me a while to learn the truth, but I'm glad that I did."

They found an empty table and after a couple of drinks relaxed into reminiscence, then more intimate topics.

Gallant stole a glance and asked, "How is your family?"

"My family is fine, nothing new there. What

about you? I heard you got married. Alaina is it?"

"Yes."

"Does married life agree with you? Are you still very much in love?" she asked with a playful smile.

"As much as possible," he said without looking at her.

Sensing he was struggling with a personal revelation, she asked gently, "Is there some . . . obstacle?"

"No. No," he said, denying the possibility. "I was referring to the burdens military life imposes on a couple."

"Ah. Good. Then you still find romance together?"

He reddened. "Yes."

"Wonderful." She wrinkled her nose. "It sounds like you've found happiness."

"And you? Have you found no one worthy of your attention?"

"I have . . . friends."

His eyebrows went up, and he started to probe deeper, but they were interrupted by the abrupt appearance of Rob Ryan at their table.

"Evening, Captain," he said, swaying a bit although his words were clear. "Can I get you a drink?"

"That's not necessary," said Gallant. He waited, but Ryan remained teetering over him.

Finally, Gallant said, "This is Lieutenant Kelsey Mitchel."

Ryan said, "Yes. I know. Kelsey and I are friends."

She asked, "Have you graduated from the academy?"

A grin spread across Ryan's face. "Damn straight!"

He pulled up a chair and sat down wearing a look like a stray dog begging for scraps at the table.

Kelsey's indulgent smile encouraged him to speak his mind. He launched into an account of his training and how great flying was and what a wonderful commanding officer Gallant was. The confessions might have continued indefinitely, but Lorelei came to the rescue.

She said, "My apologies, Captain. Lucky has been doing some celebrating after winning the Top Gun competition.

"Let's drink to that!" said Ryan, raising his half-empty glass that still managed to slop beer onto the table.

Gallant surreptitiously wiped up the mess and introduced the women to each other.

Kelsey added, "Congratulations, Ryan. When is Selection Day?"

"June 7th," said Lorelei as she corralled Ryan and started leading him away. "Come back to our table, Lucky. Everyone is waiting for you."

Kelsey smiled at the departing pilots.

"You've made quite an impression on that young man," said Gallant.

"Tomorrow he won't even remember that we talked."

Gallant's smile faded. "It won't be easy for me, knowing your squadron is assigned here."

"I could ask to be reassigned, although I

wouldn't like that. What about you?" she probed.

"Not necessarily," said Gallant, searching her face.

She leaned across the table and touched his hand. "Come visit me."

"I will," said Gallant, not even trying to disguise his eagerness.

"Soon?"

CHAPTER 9

The Loneliest Outpost

Captain James Steward's Marine recon company occupied the loneliest outpost in the galaxy. It stood on the highest peak on a mountain range of the only habitable region of a Mars-like planet called Charlie in the Ross system. A lagoon of volcanic lava ran around the border of the mountains throwing up toxic gases into the wispy atmosphere. Frequent windstorms carried soot and ash that threatened to blind the Marines despite their skin-thin Kepler-armor suits.

After gathering the latest intelligence reports from the radar and optical sensors, Steward tromped back across the rocky ground toward division headquarters.

He reported, "General . . . the Navy . . . got their ass kicked."

"How bad?"

"Bad . . . sir. Six battlecruisers were destroyed."

The general grimaced at the tall, lanky sandy-haired Marine. His slow, hesitant speaking style reminded the general of his travels through Virginia.

"But the enemy wasn't able to hit our troops," added Steward. "We're picking up escape pods full of wounded. The estimated navy casualties are over . . . six thousand dead."

Stone-faced, the general said, "It's a tribute to the courage and sacrifice of those men and women in uniform. They did what was expected—when the shooting started—they faced the enemy and put everything on the line."

Steward nodded; his countenance miserable.

The 2nd Marine Division consisted of about 100 officers and 16000 enlisted. Its commander was Brigadier General William 'Bulldog' McIntyre. He had stationed one battalion at each of the two outer planets. The rest were at the main base on the third planet where he maintained his headquarters.

McIntyre rubbed his chin and asked, "How much gear was landed?"

"Not enough, sir. There are food and water for several months, but ammunition is limited."

"Technology equipment?"

"We'll be able to get the abandoned Titan space station operational."

"Heavy weapons?"

"There are some heavy weapons, but again, not enough if we're on our own long-term."

"It won't be long-term," said McIntyre, setting

his jaw.

"Butler's bugged out with every ship, sir."

"I know."

"You think that he's going to come back after the mess he's left?"

"Not Butler," said McIntyre, shaking his head.

"Who then?"

"Admiral Collingsworth will send help. He won't strand us here." Bulldog's faith resounded in his voice.

"He had better send someone . . . good. This Titan attack was a hit and run operation, but they'll be back."

"I know. They want this star system as part of a buffer zone around their home-world. Right now, we're a thorn in their side. That's why we have to hold on at all cost."

"Do you have a plan, sir?" asked Steward.

Bulldog said, "Not yet, but when you're in a no-win situation, you reassess, and you adjust strategy. You keep fighting until either you get a better outcome . . . or you die."

At that moment, Steward thought of his sister.

I might not be around to protect you, Lorelei.

The Marines prepared for the next attack. They took over the Titan space station, activating a fighter squadron for defense. They laid down a minefield along the most likely approaches to the planet and deployed drones. But messages from fleet command were vague about sending help.

The 12th Artillery Battalion held the artillery on the bleak mountain outpost, and they expected to face the brunt of any attack. The planetary defense consisted of four heavy weapon batteries. One was on the space station, and the other three were spread around the main ground base. Each battery had a half a dozen plasma guns and two missile launchers within fortified bunkers. The weapons were sighted for specific orbit ranges. The Marine units remained in underground bunkers.

Steward's reconnaissance company spotted for the artillery. The battalion commander considered Steward his right-hand man because, "While some men prayed, Steward put his faith in his gun."

The Marines knew what was coming.

Then... *it came.*

First, a wave of sixty Titan fighter-bombers came over the planet in tight vee formation.

The fighters were launched and engaged the enemy.

The Titan waves kept coming in vees that dove through the atmosphere and bombed the defenders. Strafing runs killed many more. After their assault, the fighter-bombers left. They had done considerable damage. Despite the stubborn defense and thick flak, most of the Titan craft escaped with only minor damage.

The Marines worked all the next day restoring their defenses, but the reprieve didn't last long. Follow-up waves of bombers continued the pummeling over the next few days. Marine fighters pursued and engaged with the attackers, scoring several kills, but they couldn't stop the onslaught.

Then a drone reported approaching enemy warships. There were several cruisers and a half dozen destroyers leading a group of transport assault ships.

The Titan cruisers commenced firing at long range. They targeted the space station first, then shifted to the main ground base facilities and depots.

The Marines took a licking, while General McIntyre fumed, and held his fire.

In one sally, the artillery battalion headquarters took a direct hit that killed all senior officers, leaving Steward the ranking officer. As he took command and prepared the battalion's missile and plasma artillery, he looked to Pappy for support.

Sergeant Ernie Papias was called 'Pappy' by his young recruits. He was a seasoned veteran. His long strides marked him as a man who went places in a hurry. His black hair had traces of grey along the edges, but his powerful physique filled out his uniform. Once when Steward reviewed Pappy's service record, he found that Pappy had more ribbons than the Kansas State Fair.

All that day the Titans fired railguns and missiles from a high orbit over the planet. The high-velocity metal slugs struck facilities with devastating impact. The fortifications buckled under the hard steel plunging from above.

Finally, as the Titans moved closer to the planet, McIntyre radioed Steward, "It's time. Commence firing."

From the remains of his command post on the mountain peak, Steward selected groups of weapons to fire in unison at point-blank range. He ordered, "Fire!"

Targeting the lead ship, Pappy ran to the weapons battery to check the missile launchers. Then he keyed the plasma cannon and pressed the ignition button.

Luck favored them. The first missile barrage damaged the lead warship. Pappy's aim proved true, and soon an additional hit was scored.

Steward continued to direct fire, and the next salvo hit a second destroyer.

The men cheered as Pappy moved throughout the command, getting orders translated into action.

Steward remained in the fort's control center which was still the main target of the enemy. He changed the firing sequence. Pappy's vigor stimulated the gun teams, and their fire became more effective, but the Titan return fire was devastating.

Steward had weapons stop firing when the ship targeted their vicinity. He shifted to others, but once the enemy thought those weapons had been disabled, he returned them to service.

He launched a barrage of missiles that hit the cruiser flagship while mines struck several destroyers. The Titans were in disarray. They stopped firing and moved to a higher orbit.

The men responded to this reprieve with a cheer. Steward looked like a miracle worker.

Once the warships reached a stable firing position, they began battering the planet once more.

Pappy moved a mobile battery from site to site keeping up a writhing fire while dodging enemy return fire.

Steward continued to bait and switch his fire for as long as his weapons lasted. After several hours of this cat and mouse game, a series of bursts from the warships found their mark.

In an eruption of light and noise, many of the heavy weapons were reduced to red-hot slag. When Steward opened his eyes, he lay on the ground looking up at the sky. It was several minutes before he was able to struggle to his feet. His skull felt as if it were split in two and warm blood trickled down his left ear and cheek. He dismissed the pain and stood up.

Pappy came running to his side.

Steward yelled, "This is hell!"

In response, Pappy quipped, "The only way to get out of hell is to keep marching forward."

So, they kept firing.

After a while, the artillery had destroyed, or crippled, two cruisers and several destroyers.

The Titan force had had enough and began to withdraw. Their assault transport turned around and never came close to the planet.

The Marine fighter swept in and scored several hits on the assault ships.

The entire Titans force withdrew in hasty confusion.

Steward said, "We've driven them off for now.

But make no mistake, they'll be back."

"I hope the navy gets the message that we could use some help here," said Pappy. "I think we've used up the last of our trick plays."

A few days later, Gallant submitted a report to the President, via the Secretary of Defense.

> Mr. President,
> I've given my evaluation report on the first and second battles in the Ross System to Secretary Gilbert. I have included specific details to support my findings, but I would like to highlight a few of the most pressing conclusions in this letter.
>
> 1. The enemy's precipitous retreat from Admiral Butler in the first battle and the Marines' success in driving off the second assault force with minimal resources suggests a larger purpose. They could be using the Marines as bait to trap a relief fleet.
> 2. Whether this is the case, or not, I recommend that a strong fleet of new construction ships under the sure and able command of Admiral Collingsworth be deployed ASAP to escort a relief convoy to Ross. This will ensure the Marines are relieved with minimal concern for an enemy ambush.

3. New construction ships should be pri-
    oritized over repairs and renovation of
    other ships.

I am available to respond to specifics as you
require.

Respectfully yours,

Henry Gallant
Henry Gallant, Captain, UPN
P.S. I've taken the liberty of forwarding a
copy of my report to Admiral Collingsworth.

CHAPTER 10
Selection Day

June 7th was Selection Day at the Top Gun Academy—always a jubilant occasion. It was the night graduates had the opportunity to mold their destiny by selecting their homeport and first ship. It was like a football draft; only here, the players chose their team.

The auditorium resounded with music and cheers as friends and family joined the officers in celebration. As Top Gun, this was Ryan's night. Top Gun had been his goal for as long as he could remember. But having no family to share the moment, left him with a hollow victory. He moped through the crowd of pilots with their loved ones.

He saw a friend and asked, "Dusty, what took you so long to get here?"

"I'm sorry, Lucky. My family monopolized my time. That's why I didn't make it to the Top Gun party last night."

Flannery approached the pair and cracked a grin. "Don't sweat it. Without you there, Lucky managed to hook up with a terrific brunette."

"Who?"

"Kelsey Mitchel."

"You hooked up with Kelsey?"

Ryan shrugged, trying to appear noncommittal. "She's a sweet kid. I ran into her at the club, and we hit it off."

"She's mighty fine."

Ryan said, "It just worked out."

"Nice. You're a real player," said Flannery.

He spoke loud enough to be heard by a group standing nearby—including Lorelei.

Shamefaced, Ryan said, "We had a few drinks and pleasant conversation. I said we should get together again, and she agreed. That's all that happened."

Lorelei turned away, visibly upset.

The pilot's excitement returned to the ceremony. The front wall of the hall was covered with white placards listing every available squadron billet in the Solar System.

The pilots knew that after Selection Day, their next assignments would be at the discretion of the service to even out the quality spread. Quality spread meant that every squadron needed top-notch people, even if some locations were less desirable.

Over the loudspeaker, they heard, "Officers should take this opportunity to consider a training command. Our future aviators are determined in large part by the quality of their instruction. We encourage you to consider joining our staff here at the Academy."

Names would be called by performance rank.

So, they knew, 'If you want your number one choice, be number one.'

Ship captains vied to induce the best of the best to select their ship. They roamed among the pilots offering liberties and benefits as incentives to join their ships based on Earth, Mars, Jupiter, or Saturn.

The captain of the carrier, *Glorious,* grabbed Ryan's arm. "Rob, I want to tell you about the liberal policies on *Glorious.* They will make your tenure not only a successful career builder but a rewarding experience."

Ryan listened without enthusiasm.

Soon it was time for selection.

The loudspeaker roared, "Rob Ryan. Top Gun of this class!"

Ryan walked forward.

Dusty smacked him on the back.

Flannery yelled, "Hoot! Hoot!"

When Ryan reached the wall, he stared as if he were unprepared. Finally, he took the placard for the

6th Fighter Squadron on the *Constellation.* He hoisted it over his head like a trophy and wondered if selecting Kelsey's ship was foolish.

The selection process continued. When their names were called, each pilot marched to the wall. There was celebration and joy as each officer stepped up. It was quite a spectacle. They were having a great time shouting and waving their arms.

One pilot chose a ship in New Annapolis, Mars, near his hometown, which sounded good to him.

Another pilot laughed. "I've never been there. I've heard good things."

Someone commented, "And a little scary."

Then the announcer called, "Lorelei Steward."

Lorelei rose and walked to the front wall. She picked the placard for the 8th Fighter-bomber Squadron on the *Constellation*.

Amid the press of celebration, Ryan caught Lorelei's eye, and a look passed between them. The sudden pang he felt was swept away by the anticipation of the adventure to come. They would be on the same ship.

He watched her long stride and swaying hips as she walked across the room. He was mesmerized by the undulating motion. When she looked back, she caught his stare and gave him a knowing smile. Then with one more step, her figure vanished into the crowd.

He got up and crossed the room. He found her sitting alone in a dark, secluded table in the back corner of the room.

She looked stunning. Her oval face, green eyes, and long flowing red hair were complemented by the warmth of her vivacious teasing smile.

"It looks like we'll be shipmates," he said, without hinting if he found that idea attractive.

She said, "You have marvelous powers of observation. I doubt that anything escapes you. An essential asset for a pilot."

"You mock me, but I do have other qualities I

could claim."

"Such as?"

"I'm Top Gun," he said with a self-satisfied grin.

"Your modesty does you proud."

He shrugged off her dig as he swallowed the last of his drink. "I need a refill. Can I get you one?"

"Manhattan."

"Coming right up."

A few minutes later, he returned with the drinks to find her talking gaily with several young men. When she spotted him, she waved, flashing a happy smile.

"You've come!" said Lorelei, patting the seat next to her. The other men lingered until it became clear they were wasting their time.

"Your Manhattan," he said, pushing the drink in front of her.

They clinked glasses.

Lorelei took a sip, licked her lips, and gave him a coy glance. "What do you think your future holds?"

"I'm not a fortune-teller."

"Can't you guess?"

Her question triggered a childhood memory of when he asked his mother what he would be when he grew up. She laughed and sang merrily, "*Que Sera Sera.*"

He looked at Lorelei and said, "Whatever will be, will be."

She frowned at his lack of candor.

He asked, "What about you?"

"My earliest dreams have always been about going to the stars," she said with a faraway look on her face.

He blinked. "A lofty ambition for a child, but you made those dreams come true."

"We both have," she smiled warmly.

He said, "It's been a glorious day."

"Yes. I propose a toast."

He raised his glass to hers.

Her eyes lit up as she beamed at him. "To the Top Gun."

Feeling extraordinarily pleased with himself, he chugged the drink.

Lorelei reached across the table and touched his hand.

They kissed.

CHAPTER 11

The Invitation

"We've received an invitation," said Gallant, his eyes wide with surprise as he passed the message to his wife.

Alaina read out loud, "'Fleet Admiral George F. Collingsworth invites Captain and Mrs. Henry Gallant to attend the commissioning ceremony for the Spacecraft Carrier *Constellation*. Wednesday, June 14th, at 1600 hours.' Why were we invited?"

"Probably because many of my students chose to serve on the *Constellation*."

"Hmmm. I have no idea what I should wear to such an event," said Alaina. "Who can I ask?"

But Gallant was already lost in thought taking in the implications of the invitation.

"How do I look?" asked Alaina twirling to show

off the luxurious folds of her formal evening dress.

The designer gown had cost a small fortune, but Gallant was delighted with the effect. The raven-black strapless dress had a plunging V-neck and a body-hugging fit. A cutaway front panel in the fluted skirt gave a tantalizing glimpse of Alaina's shapely legs as she spun.

"Perfection," beamed Gallant. "You'll be the most attractive woman there."

His reward was a kiss on the cheek.

He caught a flash of his reflection in the mirror, startled at how distinguished he looked.

I look older. Am I any wiser?

Alaina said, "Full-dress suits you."

He felt a rush of pleasure at her praise. He liked wearing 'blues.' Full-dress was like service dress with the exception that full-size medals were worn above the left breast pocket instead of ribbons.

For the finishing touch, he buckled on a ceremonial pearl-handled sword.

"Shall we go?"

"Yes, Dear," said Alaina, linking her arm through his while giving him an approving smile.

Soon they were flying from Melbourne to the *Constellation*. They were accompanied by elegantly dressed dignitaries from all over the Solar System.

The shuttlecraft had an expansive view of the space-station shipyard which was floating over Earth. The shipyard was a city unto itself with a population of over 40,000 workers and residents. It enclosed two kilometers of corridor at its core with twenty-four docks spiraling outward. Each dock supported a ship as large as a battlecruiser. The *Constellation* was in docking bay seven next to the mighty dreadnought *Victory.*

As they waited at the gangway, Alaina tugged on the duty officer's tunic and pointed at an approaching dinghy with distinctive markings.

"Who's that?"

"I don't know for sure, Madam, but the scuttlebutt is some top brass."

He was right.

Admiral Collingsworth stepped into the entry port to a flurry of salutes. He returned the salutes and turned to wait as the president's yacht approached.

Commander Margret Fletcher, the ship's construction supervisor, took the distinguished visitors on a tour.

As the president enjoyed the tour, people swirled around him talking gaily. He put on a little show greeting various officers and men and chatted about their families before he disappeared below decks.

Gallant was only half-listening to the conversation when a shimmer of light caught his eye—looking past the bright lights and a sea of faces—he saw Kelsey. His vision narrowed until she was all he could see. She wore a gold silk gown that accentuated her hazelnut hair. Her bare arms and graceful neck glowed with a warm tan. After several moments, he realized that Alaina was tugging on his sleeve.

"Henry? Henry!"

With difficulty, he turned his gaze away and said, "Sorry, Alaina, I was . . . thinking."

At that moment, Kelsey walked up to him.

"Hello, Henry," she said pleasantly.

"Kelsey. I'm . . . hmmm," he stammered. "I'm surprised to see you here."

"My father-in-law dragged me here to show support for his political ambitions. He's here because the president chose to make an appearance."

Kelsey turned to Gallant's wife and said, "Alaina, I'm so happy to meet you. Henry has spoken highly of you."

Her perfume enveloped him as she spoke. Standing between two such women, his thoughts threatened to spin out of control.

"Has he now?" asked Alaina, arching her eyebrows at her husband.

Kelsey's presence was intoxicating, but Alaina's sharp tone snapped him back to reality. Realizing he needed to tread carefully, he started to answer, but Kelsey beat him to it.

"We had a few drinks at the *Liftoff* last week. He talked expansively about you."

"You had a few drinks, did you?" asked Aliana, turning to Gallant. "Funny, I don't remember you mentioning that."

Alaina patted Gallant's left arm with one hand as the other slid behind him. He barely managed to suppress a jump when she pinched the back of his arm. Hard.

He clamped his lips together, dismayed to realize that the pinch was nothing compared to what he could expect when he got home. He averted his gaze from Kelsey.

Gallant was so lost in his thoughts that he didn't notice that the commissioning ceremony had begun. Soon the ceremony was complete, and the guests started the evening festivities. A sit-down dinner was in the large mess hall. The tables were covered with fine lace linen with centerpieces of ice sculptured ships. Each table was adorned with flowers separating the serving platters.

To Gallant's dismay, he and Alaina were seated at the same table with Gerome Neumann and Kelsey.

To keep his eyes off Kelsey, Gallant focused his attention on Agatha Turnbull, Graves' chief of staff, who sat opposite him at the round table. She was a large-boned woman with plump red cheeks—the antithesis of both the elegant Kelsey and the lovely Alaina.

With a start, he heard the waiter at his elbow ask his wine preference.

"I'll drink along with Captain Turnbull," he said, choosing the safest option.

Kelsey said, "I would like to congratulate you, Henry, on the outstanding graduation of your class."

Gallant mumbled his thanks as she rose and proposed a toast to the pilot's success.

After the toast, an army of waiters trotted out to serve the meal. Without thinking, Gallant took a large gulp of soup, gasping and blinking hard as the hot liquid hit his lips and tongue. He grabbed his wine glass to douse the burn and swigged several mouth-fuls—much more than he should have.

He heard a suppressed snicker. "The sherry must be quite good," someone commented.

Unaware of his distress, Alaina and Kelsey kept up a chatting commentary about the clashing décor color scheme, the cuisine (chicken again?), and the Navy flair for putting on a good show.

"Henry, would you pass the duck, please?" asked Kelsey. "Alaina, you should try the roast chicken. It's delicious."

He handed the plate of carved duck across the table, adding nothing to his plate. To his surprise, Alaina scooped heaps of chicken onto it. He didn't dare look at her.

Feeling gauche and out of place, he glanced around the table, studying each face to see if anyone noticed his awkwardness. He fiddled with his food, pushing things around on the plate but eating lit-tle. When the dinner plates were cleared, and dessert brought out, he ignored the fatty sweets and only picked at the fruit and cheese. While he had no appe-tite, he drank copious amounts of wine.

During a noisy moment, Gallant's dinner was interrupted when Gerome Neumann leaned over the table. He looked like he had hit the jackpot when he stared into Gallant's eyes, "You and I have unfinished business."

Neumann paused. His face clouded. "The day will come when I will be able to give you what you so richly deserve."

Gallant sat stunned as Neumann abruptly left and walked away.

He was lost in thought when a few minutes later, Admiral Collingsworth appeared at Alaina's side.

The admiral said, "Mrs. Gallant, please let me steal your husband for a little while. There is someone who wants to talk to him."

"Certainly," replied Alaina smoothly, but he saw turmoil in her face.

Gallant followed the admiral to the president's entourage. At the sight of Red, he thought,

At last, a friendly face!

Red said, "The president wants to talk with you in private. Please follow me, sir."

Gallant and the Admiral entered the *Constellation's* flag officer's suite. They waited for several minutes before he heard, "Admiral. Henry. Come in."

The president clapped the admiral on the shoulder. "George, make yourself comfortable."

Then he turned to Gallant and said, "Hello there, Henry. How about some tea? I love tea on a busy day like this." Without waiting for an answer, he pressed a button, and three glasses of iced tea materialized from the console.

"Listen to this report," said Kent. The recording gave a rundown of the latest intelligence on the Ross system.

"Your crystal ball proved accurate about Ross. Once again."

"I told you what a valuable asset this young

man is, Mr. President," said Collingsworth.

The president nodded.

Gallant said, "Mr. President, the Titans didn't defeat Admiral Butler because they were better sailors. They won because they had better technology. The new construction ships will level that playing field and give our men and women an even chance. That's all we need to beat them. We already have the will."

As he talked, the president sipped his tea and nodded.

"I found your detailed proposal for a relief effort to be helpful. Though Fleet Headquarters has its own ideas."

Collingsworth said, "You know I disagree with headquarters on this matter, Mr. President."

"Yes, you're in Gallant's camp. No argument there. Whatever we do must be along the lines of Henry's recent recommendations. And that means reinforcing Graves' 3rd Fleet. From there, our force can mount an effective sortie into Ross with supplies for the Marines."

"Mr. President, I request to head that mission," asked Admiral Collingsworth.

The president chuckled, "Not a chance George. I need you here protecting the good people of this star system. I have confidence in Admiral Graves. He'll get the job done. For now, I want to talk about these battle results and the new aliens we've discovered. For a month, strategic planners have been considering the consequences of contacting the aliens. If we locate their home star, what does your crystal ball tell you how they'll react?"

Gallant said, "I agree with much of the plan, but there are some problems."

"Then let's hear them. That's why you're here."

"If we find them compatible to work together with us, there will be critical issues. Such as do we support their efforts by offering to give them equipment and technology? That could fall into the Titans' hands."

The president said, "We can replace equipment within a year or two, but replacing men takes a generation. I'm for letting the aliens fight and kill as many Titans as possible. We want to encourage that. The more Titans they get, the fewer casualties we'll take."

Gallant said, "Moving large numbers of men and equipment to the front is a logistic nightmare. It's the same for them. It takes ships and time for major deployments. What if we move in the wrong direction while the Titans make a counter move?"

The admiral nodded, "Defense has serious advantages. We have a huge problem. The titanium needed to build more ships alone is astronomical."

"Are you saying we'll never have the ships to carry out an invasion of the Titan home system?" asked the president.

"That's a possibility, despite the optimism of fleet headquarters," concluded the admiral.

Gallant said, "We can only guess how long the aliens have been at war, but I'm guessing centuries.

It takes time to travel and fight over lightyear distances."

"I see," said the president sitting back for a moment. Then he leaned forward and grabbed Gallant's arm. "On another note, I've kept you shuttling around at my disposal long enough. What do you say to a new command?"

"I'd love that, Mr. President. I'll take whatever hulk is available."

"Hulk nothing. You've earned a first-class command, and I'll see you get it." He turned toward Collingsworth. "That is if you think I have any influence with the admiralty?"

Admiral Collingsworth laughed. "You can send Gallant wherever you like."

Kent turned back to Gallant. "You told me you would like to take part in the relief force to Ross. And I'm pleased to give you a support position under Admiral Graves."

"Me, sir?"

"Yes, you. George recommended you and . . . well, what do you think of the *Constellation*?"

"She's a fine ship. I'd be thrilled with a post aboard her."

"Just a post? What about commanding her?"

Gallant had to stop himself from leaping to his feet. "I think I can do that, Mr. President."

"You think you can? Don't you know?"

"I can!"

"Well, you've spent enough time on the beach, and I owe you a debt for your counsel."

"Thank you, Mr. President."

Winking at the admiral, Kent asked, "Do you approve?"

"I do wholeheartedly."

"Mr. Gallant, you will assume command of the *Constellation* and spearhead the relief force to Ross. I have high expectations for you."

Gallant managed to stammer, "Thank you again, Mr. President. I won't let you down."

CHAPTER 12

The Constellation

Gallant's shoulders tightened as he saluted the flag and asked, "Request permission to come aboard, sir?"

Pride welled up in his chest as he took command of the *Constellation* minutes later.

As the ultimate weapon in space, the spacecraft carrier combined power and grandeur. The carrier accommodated ninety spacecraft and featured a flight deck with four launchers. Twice the size of a battlecruiser, at full combat load she displaced 160,000 tons and was propelled by both interplanetary and warp engines. Her armament bristled with missiles, plasma weapons, and laser cannons. She was equipped with an armor belt and force shield plus electronic warfare decoys. The ship's communication, navigation, and sensors boasted state-of-the-art AI. Her stealth capability, though limited, minimized detectable signals.

It was easy to step aboard his new ship and expect everything to be perfectly shipshape, but he knew better. Once in his stateroom, Captain Henry Gallant read his orders for the third time.

From: Commander-in-Chief United Planets Fleet
To: Captain Henry Gallant
Subj: Ship Assignment
Ref: (a) BuPers Order UP 066704 (b) Ops File

1. Under Reference (a) Captain Henry Gallant is directed to assume command of UPSS *Constellation* CVS-647 and make all preparation for deployment within 30 days.
2. When directed, *Constellation* is to be attached to Third Fleet under Vice Admiral Graves for operations in hostile territory as per attached Reference (b).
3. Report for duty Friday, June 16th, 0800 hours.
4. No delay is authorized.

George Forsyth Collingsworth
Fleet Admiral George Forsyth Collingsworth
Commander-in-Chief, United Planets Fleet

"Blast it all! Thirty days? That's impossible."

Thirty days until deployment meant he had two weeks to complete last-minute construction details, including testing and calibration. Then a week for a shakedown cruise to wring out the bugs followed by a week to fix everything that they found that needed fixing.

"Damn it! It's just not possible."

It was his pessimistic nature to assume the situation was precariously balanced to force himself to find a way forward. Though it hardly seemed likely that he could change this unrealistic directive into a workable plan.

He still had to recruit officers and men to fill the remaining billets. His reputation was pitted against more distinguished captains. A dozen more ship's officers and pilots, along with several score enlisted men and women were needed. But most of all, he wanted to convince two Top Gun pilots to take on the responsibility of squadron leaders.

Besides personnel shortages, he faced equipment installation and calibration requirements. He had a disappointing experience while commissioning his last ship and knew that appealing to the shipyard master wouldn't be of much help. Other ship berths were already swarming with activity. Battle damaged ships were being hauled into empty docks. Workers and military personnel hustled about the yard.

He had a conversation with the shipyard steward whose sour face matched his tedious position. The steward was a senior engineer working for the NNR corporation. He was a sparse man with gray hair and a well-trimmed beard. He represented the key shipyard associates that would decide how to allocate the scant resources.

The NRR man said, "Over the last year, I worked with Commander Fletcher to construct this superb ship. I've worked out the costs and workforce requirements so as not to overtax our fragile budget. Thanks to the generosity of Mr. Gerome Neumann, President of the NNR Corporation, credit and major equipment procurement won't be a problem."

When Gallant examined the actual allocations, he feared the effort would fall short.

Yet, something had to be done.

Failure to meet his roster or to complete space trials would mean swift loss of his command and shore duty for the rest of his career. He had no illusion of garnering support from the admiralty. Admiral Graves would welcome any opportunity to deny him a billet in the Third Fleet.

Even with all these considerations, the duty officer kept pestering Gallant with trivial problems.

Doesn't he realize his captain had more important business to attend to?

Irritably, Gallant scratched his head. Too restless to remain in his cabin, he picked up his schedule tablet and went for a walk about the ship. It gave him some small satisfaction to see men jump out of his way as he marched through the deck wearing a frightful scowl. The sight of his ill-tempered frown left no doubt that he was not to be troubled.

Men were completing tasks with wartime urgency. Crewmen went over inventory lists and stored items. They loaded commodities such as food, ammunition, fuel, and hydraulic oil. Along the overstuffed passageways, workers moved equipment. He stopped to watch a crane hoisting out scaffolding. When he examined the welding and the rigging, there was an acetone stench in the air.

To lighten his mood, he stopped and took a deep breath, closing his eyes for a moment. When he opened them, he focused on the *Constellation's* elegant curves, sleek finish, and exceptional fighting qualities. He turned and strode into the weapons bay, where workers were installing the missile launchers and plasma blasters. But everyone he passed seemed to watch him out of the corner of their eyes, wary of invoking his wrath.

Loose gear lay tangled on the deck and miscellaneous fittings lay about. Gallant confronted a workman who was careless and allowed a hauling line to go slack and crash a machine.

"Blast it all! Can't anyone do a job right? Look at this mess. Where's your chief?"

He was in no mood to be chatty as the engineering chief approached with a cheerful, "Good morning, Captain."

"Harrumph," he sputtered and pointed. "Get this mess in proper order."

Gallant turned on his heel and stalked into the next compartment, almost running into the executive officer.

"Good morning, sir," said Margret Fletcher. She had a lean face with a hawksbill nose and a no-nonsense air of strict compliance to regs, but no visible personality.

She said, "I have the latest personnel status report."

Gallant examined the numbers and growled, "Why haven't we received our quota of recruits?"

The XO shrugged and shifted her feet.

"You should've been on top of this. It's a high priority to bring the crew to full strength."

She shrugged again with an air of unconcern. Gallant's assignment to the *Constellation* had irked quite a few officers, and one of those unhappy people was Margret Fletcher. She had taken the ship through shipyard construction and had expected to be its captain.

"Harrumph," muttered Gallant. He was not a captain who would accept half-hearted efforts from his officers and had already formed an unfavorable opinion of her.

He wondered how he could win her over to his side.

"XO, join me on an inspection tour of the engineering spaces."

"Aye aye, Captain."

They traversed the ship from fore to aft, noting problems that only added to Gallant's concern. The lax standards and slackers he saw enraged him. He knew in times of crisis those weak links couldn't be relied on, and too often others paid the price.

He was convinced the XO would not meet his high standards.

◆ ◆ ◆

Later that day, Gallant sat in his ready room, compiling a schedule for completing deployment preparations. He knew the ship was incomplete and needed the expertise of his officers to identify conflicting demands and activities. The next step was to call his officers to the wardroom so he could take their measure and motivate them to work with him to prepare the ship for space trials.

As he settled into his chair at the head of the table, he noticed a plaque inscribed "UP *Constellation* UPSS 647" hanging on the wall. He felt a rush of pride at being her captain. He gazed around the wardroom. Fletcher took a seat between the weapons officer and Lieutenant Commander Thomas Harris, the ship's engineer. Each held a mug of coffee in one hand and a tablet in the other. They exchanged furtive glances while examining their department's list of needs.

At the last minute, Midshipman Daniel Logan scurried in and fell into a seat at the foot of the table. The youngest member of the wardroom, Logan exuded a somewhat annoying air of innocence and boundless enthusiasm.

"Go on, Daniel," said Harris, the grizzled older man in a disheveled uniform with grease stains in odd places. "You were telling us about your engineering training at the academy."

With a lively good-natured smile, Daniel began spouting basic engineering to the ship's engineering expert.

Realizing how much experience was in the room, he blushed to the tips of his ears. "I mean, I've got a lot to learn, but I'm ready to do my part."

There were a few good-natured chuckles around the table.

Harris rubbed his hands together. "I'm ready to help you."

The weapons officer snickered, stretching his lanky legs under the table. He tugged at his thick non-reg hair. "The engineer has his methods which you'll soon learn."

Gallant stopped the chatter cold. "Officers, I called you here to discuss the daunting schedule we face."

He distributed his outline and requirements, watching each officer's face as they browsed through.

The engineer said, "Captain, I agree it's essential for us to get the planning process right. Otherwise, we'll go off half-cocked."

The talk shifted to technical production needs. He outlined what materials and equipment would be required to complete the ship's installations.

Next came discussion on the preparation of missiles and weapons.

The weapons officer said, "This is a damnable schedule. I don't know how I'll get it all done. The loading and prepping of the fighters alone ..."

Gallant stood and leaned forward with his hands on the polished table. "I hate this schedule as much as you do, but there's a war on, and we must meet the admiral's timetable for deployment. In my judgment, we'll succeed if we start with a methodical plan that we all commit to. Then execution will go smoother."

Fletcher said, "I've been working on a system to coordinate the schedule across all departments. It should be ready in a few days."

Gallant said, "We're all present now. Let's proceed in an orderly manner. We can get assignments and people moving immediately. First, each of you examine your schedule requirements right now and tell me of any glaring conflicts."

Fletcher bristled, "I would like to have the department heads review this schedule over several days. They can provide comments to me and then I could make final revisions."

"No. We will discuss the overlapping interference issues and major problem areas here and now. We will not leave this room until we can all agree it is possible to meet each assignment."

Fletcher fidgeted as she said, "Why hasn't anyone submitted these requirements to me ahead of time so I could have worked them out. Now I'll have to redo ..."

"This is why I want to vet this schedule now, Commander. To iron out these discrepancies before we get going at full speed."

"I'm afraid, I must meet with each department head and redo everything," she insisted.

Gallant rolled his eyes. He guessed that Fletcher was the kind of paper-pusher who would file a complaint with fleet headquarters.

The operations officer said, "I have some ideas for training and maintenance schedules. But I'm afraid it'll mean pulling people away from their assignments."

Harris said, "What? You shouldn't schedule training until I've completed installations and checks."

"I need to get a block of time that will require some power limitation," said the operations officer.

Harris said, "You know we're on a tight leash here. Fleet has its demands for space trials, and I need to run proficiency tests on the engines. That could impact plans for upgrading the AI software."

Gallant said, "I want to get started right away. We've limited time, and I have prepared a testing programming and training regimen to get the ship and crew off the mark. XO you need to get shipyard to bring on stores and spacecraft later."

"The personnel requirements will not be met," objected Fletcher.

Something about her voice grated on Gallant's nerves. She was upsetting to his sense of order. He said, "I understand you have prohibited Harris from starting the calibration tests."

"No, sir."

He glared at her. "No, you didn't prohibit him, or no, he can't start."

"I couldn't allow him to proceed with his work because of the loading..."

The gentle, soothing tone of her voice, as if she

were addressing a backward child, infuriated him further.

"Engine testing is a higher priority because we can only do that with the dock facilities. Rearranging stores can be done once we've started space trials."

"That is contrary to regulations. I am trying to *help* you stay within the regs."

"We must improvise to meet our departure time. That means cutting corners where we can, and realize which things cannot be shortchanged, such as engine testing."

"But the regulations..."

"Commander, you are failing to recognize this ship's priorities."

"Sir, I'm trying to meet a tight schedule, and I must protest your interference with the proper procedure."

He clenched his fists. Boiling with exasperation, he said, "This is my ship. I say what is, and what is not proper procedure."

"Sir, the safety of this ship requires that we follow regulations as written."

"Commander," said Gallant, his face turning crimson, "I'm the ultimate authority about the safety of this ship. Is that clear?"

Unconvinced and unrepentant, the XO mumbled, "I must repeat, regulations state..."

Seeing her ready to be unhelpful, yet again, he wanted to steamroll past her and slam his fist onto the table. Instead, he took a moment to bury his emotions.

Calmly, he said, "This deployment is part of 3rd Fleet's mission to relieve the Marines in the Ross system."

He let that sink in. His gaze flew around the room, catching the eyes of every officer present.

Finally, he said, "This ship . . . *will not let those Marines down.*"

CHAPTER 13

Squadron Leaders

G allant's stateroom aboard the *Constellation* didn't feel like home. It was more like a hotel celebrity suite than a man-cave. And he didn't think he would ever get used to the Marine stationed outside his door.

Since the perpetual motion of crew and machines required the judicious touch of the carrier's captain, he was never off duty. So, a second smaller cabin near the bridge was available for his convenience. With only a bed and a desk, it was like the cabin he had enjoyed on his first ship. His cot abutted the wall and stretched the length of the room. It had a display monitor embedded into the wall over the bed that could show video of any location within the ship. This screen could also list every vital ship parameter whenever he called upon the AI. A desk and dresser cabinet filled the corner farthest from the door. A table with two chairs were the last pieces of furniture. All the furnishings were simple, unadorned items that suited Gallant's practical taste. He considered the tiny cabin to be an affluent luxury, a piece of incomparable good fortune, a gifted sanctuary that fitted his nature, so he preferred conducting the ship's affairs there.

On his second day as the commanding officer of the *Constellation*, he was buried in reports about the progress, or rather the lack thereof, in deployment preparations. He ran his hand through his hair as he examined each new problem.

If only the XO wouldn't fight me at every turn.

A knock on his door interrupted him.

"Enter."

Lorelei took two steps inside and stood at attention. "Ensign Steward, reporting as ordered, sir."

Gallant noticed her pale green eyes squinting in the light but continued to work at his desk.

A minute later, there was another rap.

"Enter."

"Ensign Ryan, reporting as ordered, sir."

Still, Gallant said nothing. Although he appeared to be ignoring them, he noticed Ryan steal a questioning look at Lorelei. She squinted and gave the faintest shrug. They looked like delinquent children waiting in the principal's office.

Gallant suppressed an urge to laugh at their antics.

Soon a third rap sounded.

"Enter."

"You wanted to see me, Captain?" asked Lieutenant Kelsey Mitchel.

Gallant put his work aside and stood up. He said, "At ease."

The small cabin was now very crowded.

"Harrumph," muttered Gallant. Pressing his lips together, he shifted his gaze from one to the next in turn, assessing the personal tensions between these young people.

He considered the carrier space-wing of the *Constellation.* It consisted of three squadrons; Fighter Squadron 6 had thirty-six Viper I, Fighter-Bomber Squadron 8 had thirty-six Viper II, and Recon Squadron 10 had eighteen Hawkeye.

Is this a wise choice? Can these officers lead and cooperate?

He spoke deliberately. "I've chosen you three to be squadron leader of your respective squadrons."

"Wow!" said Ryan.

Lorelei and Kelsey exchanged smiles.

"You're all talented pilots," said Gallant. "Your skill is a gift, an ability so natural that you don't realize how hard things become when something goes wrong. And something always goes wrong. That's what I want you to realize."

The puzzled stares he received made him add, "Your job as a leader will be more than flying. You must anticipate your squadron's needs and nurture your people. And you must be ready to deal with an unexpected change of fortune. Are you willing to undertake this responsibility?"

The three nodded as if they were already feeling the weight of their new responsibility.

"Any questions?"

He waited a few seconds and then said, "Good luck," and shook the hand of each in turn.

CHAPTER 14

Shakedown Cruise

Gallant sat in the command chair on the bridge, alert to the last-minute preparations.

After the struggle to finalize preparations, the crew was buzzing with excitement. Their first voyage aboard the *Constellation*, a one-week shakedown cruise, would test and assess everything from navigation to fighter operations.

"All maneuvering stations report manned and ready, Ma'am," reported the chief.

"Very well," said Commander Fletcher. She stepped up on the command deck and took the seat beside the captain. "Engineering, bridge; Standby to answer all bells."

"Bridge, engineering; Ready to answer all bells, Ma'am," came the crisp response over the intercom.

"Captain, the ship is ready to maneuver," said the XO.

"Very well," said Gallant, "I have the conn.

Chief, release the grappling magnets."

The chief reported, "Green board, sir."

"Helm, ahead slow."

"Aye aye, sir," responded the helmsman. "Engines answering ahead slow—fifteen meters per second and increasing."

Fletcher said, "The space tug is standing by for your orders, Captain."

Here it is . . . my first operational decision as captain of the Constellation.

Using a tug in the confined quarters of a shipyard was the prudent choice. But this ship was heading out to face dangerous challenges. Gallant didn't want to miss the opportunity to show that he was a bold leader who had confidence in his crew.

"We won't need the tug," said Gallant. "Helm, port thrusters ahead one third, come starboard five degrees."

He gazed about him. Everything on the bridge was in order. The crew was carrying out his orders, and the *Constellation* was responding well. But something was peculiar—something was unusual—something was different. Then he realized; Chief Howard, Lieutenant Roberts, nor any of his shipmates from his past ships were onboard. He had been in the navy since he was fifteen and he never knew a lonelier day than today.

Soon the *Constellation* maneuvered clear of the spaceport and away from obstructing traffic.

"Navigator plot a course to our operating area," said Gallant.

"Aye aye, sir," said the navigator. The shakedown drills would be conducted outside the Mars orbit. "Recommend course one one zero, mark two, sir."

"Helm, ahead standard, come to course one one zero, mark two," ordered Gallant.

"Aye aye, sir."

Exercises and drills went well on the first day of the cruise. But once the crew started on flight operations testing, tension escalated. The deck was a dangerous place—like a busy day at an airport in a major city, with a shorter runway and less margin for catastrophe.

The flight crew moved each fighter into position on the catapult, essentially an oversized slingshot, then raised the blast deflector behind the craft. Once the flight deck cleared, the hanger depressurized, and the doors opened to the vacuum of space. The catapult officer sprung a high-speed piston that shot the fighter into space while the pilot throttled the engine, rocketing the 90,000-kilo fighter from 0 to 100 km/s in seconds.

Recovering the fighter was even tougher. Pilots had to align their craft with the docking bay and apply reverse thrust to get zero relative velocity with a tolerance of mere centimeters before the electromagnetic tractor beam could guide the craft to a safe landing.

At normal operations, the crew could launch one fighter every two minutes—just enough time to avoid deadly collisions. Recoveries were processed five minutes apart to maintain fighter separation during their approach.

During combat, those tolerances were reduced to achieve four launches per minute, and four recovers every two minutes.

The pace was both demanding and treacherous.

Drills tested both the pilots' and the crews' abilities. But as the exercises became more exacting, minor accidents began to occur. The flight crews kept the pilots flying even as a troubling pattern emerged.

After one mishap, Gallant asked the returning pilot, "What was the problem with your ship?"

The pilot said, "Minor bugs, sir. That's all. My crew chief and I will iron them out. Nothing to be concerned about."

But Gallant was worried. The fighters came in hot and fast, in what seemed an endless loop.

Watching the recovery operations from a monitor in the control center, he suddenly tensed in his chair. He wasn't sure how he knew, but something terrible was about to happen.

A fighter came in too fast and high for the tractor beams to hold it. Alarms screamed as the craft skidded along the flight deck, careened to the side, and ricocheted off the hanger bulkhead before ramming a maintenance station. The twisted hulk finally came to rest with its nose mashed into the deck, the tail pointing straight up.

"Crash! Crash! Crash!" blared the intercom. "Attention all hands! Crash in the forward landing bay. Forward crash and rescue party, proceed to the casualty."

Gallant leapt to his feet, ready to pull on a spacesuit and lead the rescue team personally, but he forced himself to sit back down. His crew had to be able to handle emergencies on their own. Fingers digging into the chair arms, he watched Midshipman Logan and the C&R team, on standby already in spacesuits, head toward the launch bay.

Mobile bulkheads sealed the vast flight deck into smaller compartments.

The C&R chief reported, "The team is assembled. Equipment ready."

Logan steeled himself as he sealed his breathing apparatus. He coughed against the restricted airflow of his protective gear. "Follow me," he said and led the team through the airlock and into the vacuum compartment.

After several tentative steps in one direction, he backtracked around some wreckage and tried again.

Dodging a sudden shower of sparks, he shouted, "Kill all the electrical panels in this bay! Shut the isolation valves to the fuel piping."

Men scrambled to follow his orders as Logan made his way through the debris to reach the injured crew.

The team's recovery equipment allowed them to cut open the fighter and extract the pilot with minimal difficulty.

Logan reported to the OOD, "The pilot has been taken to sickbay. All crew members accounted for and retrieved."

Gallant gave an immense sigh of relief. The team had quickly and efficiently stabilized injuries, carried the crew to safety, and cleared the accident. All that remained was to determine what had gone so terribly wrong.

As soon as Gallant entered the Ready Room, the storm of angry voices died away. Most of his crew chiefs slumped in their chairs, their arms crossed and faces scowling.

He considered the crowd. "This inquiry will investigate the accidents that occurred during the shakedown. The main problems occurred with Fighter Squadron 6, but other squadrons may be affected as well."

He scanned the room, waiting for an explanation from each chief in turn.

The chief of operations said, "We were making progress, upgrading from normal to combat speed, but that's now on hold while we figure out the weak points."

"My crash teams had to deal with some dicey situations—fire and potential explosions, not to mention crew injuries," said the damage control chief.

The chief of ship handlers glared. "My handlers performed up to standard. The root of the crashes must be maintenance mistakes or calibration miscues."

"Looked like systematic data errors or operational guidance faults to me," said the maintenance chief, shaking his head.

The flight chief said, "I don't know what caused the accidents. My crew takes good care of the fighters and I know we've got good pilots. I can't pin down the problems the pilots are reporting, but mishaps keep cropping up during landing and operating. It must be something other than the ships. I'd stake my reputation on it, sir."

Gallant rubbed his forehead. "We have to be missing something."

The XO suggested, "Have you considered the possibility of sabotage? A computer virus, perhaps."

"Sabotage?" the chorus of voice responded in shock.

"I'll conduct a thorough investigation. The first thing is to reboot the AI security protocols."

Gallant gave her a hard look. "The ship is protected by more than just bulkheads and missiles. There are cameras, motion sensors, roving guards, alarm systems. Even if saboteurs could get past all that, they would need passwords and keycards. And don't forget the thumbprint scans and facial recognition."

"Considerable protection, as you say, sir. Yet people break into well-secured facilities all the time."

CHAPTER 15

Suspicion

On the last day of the shakedown cruise, Lorelei slammed open the door to the Ready Room. Shock and dismay were written across her face.

Kelsey looked up from her mission plan. "What's wrong? I thought you were conducting flight ops today."

"I was . . .," started Lorelei, her voice trailing off. Kelsey Mitchell was the last person she wanted to discuss her problem with. On the surface, the two were friendly. They shared leadership responsibilities, conducted joint training ops, and attended briefings together. But privately, Lorelei couldn't decide if Kelsey was her friend or her nemesis—and she was undoubtedly a rival for Ryan's attention.

Kelsey's rich and powerful father-in-law, not to mention her ambiguous relationship with the captain, made her something of an enigma. Still, as a fellow squadron leader, she was the natural person for Lorelei to confide in.

Lorelei continued, "I ran an accident analysis. The results shocked me."

"Oh, no. Is it getting worse?"

"I don't know . . . well, I'm not sure. I mean . . . I don't know what I mean."

"Um . . . say that again?"

Lorelei held out her arms. "Accidents in Squadrons' 8 and 10 looks typical for this stage of training; a few minor incidents, nothing major, but Squadron 6's performance was out of bounds. They've had several serious crashes. Two pilots are in the hospital along with four of the flight crew. That doesn't even include the damage from minor incidents. I don't understand how the data could be so different."

Kelsey lowered her brows. "Do you think Ryan has overtaxed his people or equipment? Maybe he's taking on more difficult assignments? Or could it be a failure of his maintenance team?"

"No. Nothing like that."

"What then? Enlighten me?"

Lorelei hesitated, then shook her head. "I took his logbook."

"You took his logbook?" The admission startled Kelsey.

"Yes."

"Let me see."

Lorelei rummaged through her flight bag and produced the logbook. She held it out gingerly as if it might bite her.

"Look here."

"Humm. How did you get this?"

Lorelei's face turned pink. "He ... uh ... he left it in my stateroom ... one night."

Kelsey's eyes went wide. "Tell me everything! And be specific, I want details."

"Not now. Look at the logbook. This is serious."

"And that isn't?"

At the look on Lorelei's face, Kelsey back-tracked. "Never mind. So, Ryan spent the night with you and forgot his logbook tablet."

Lorelei pressed her lips together and said nothing.

Kelsey flipped through the logbook. "He doesn't give any explanation for the accidents. He didn't conduct a standard review or get statements from the pilots and crews involved. He hasn't completed the data collection for the last few days. That's completely against regs."

Lowering her voice, Kelsey added, "You have to give this to the captain."

Lorelei's heart sank. "How can I? It isn't like he showed it to me. I took it without permission."

"Wait a minute; the XO should already have all the statistics from pilot and crew reports anyway?"

Lorelei bit her lower lip. "Yeah, but the squadron leader is supposed to interview pilots and reconcile discrepancies. He hasn't."

"That would be bad practice. You know how the XO is on regs."

She told herself to stay strong and resist the

urge to report him. "What can I do?"

Lorelei's attitude confused Kelsey. She said, "Why is it so difficult? You should just ask Ryan about it. He needs to stop and think about the consequences of what he's doing . . . or not doing."

"Ask him what? 'Did you fail to update your incident and accident reports? Did you fail to conduct proper review investigations? Did you fail to do your job?'" yelled Lorelei.

"Stop shouting!"

"You stop first!"

Kelsey sighed. "I'll ask him."

"No. Don't."

"This is a computer report, not a major crime. No one's died—have they?"

Lorelei took a deep breath and shook her head. "No. Not yet, but this can't continue. We have to do something."

Kelsey asked, "What has Ryan been doing?"

She tried to reconstruct events. "He spends his days in training exercises the same as us."

"Maybe he lost his logbook, and that's why it's outdated. Then he found it, but before he could update it he left it in your room."

"So, we're back to discussing my room?"

"Yeah. Let's talk about that juicy subject."

"No!" Lorelei insisted, but her voice quivered. "I mean . . . he didn't enter some data. It's no big deal."

"But why not? Was he hiding something?" asked Kelsey.

"Maybe he was just trying to fix the problem

before it got up the chain of command. To avoid trouble."

"Well, guess again. He's in about as much trouble as I can imagine. And so are you if you don't report this," said Kelsey.

"I don't want to make false accusations." She dug her fingers into her palm.

Kelsey shook her head. "How could he be so careless?"

"I know. I know," said Lorelei, her voice miserable. "I'm sorry."

"Sorry about what? Sleeping with Ryan or trusting him?"

Lorelei blushed and turned away. "It's not like that."

"What's it like, then?"

"I care about him."

"Are you in love with him?"

Lorelei was horrified to find that she had deep feelings for a man she should be running away from. In her wildest dream, she never imagined this happening.

What's wrong with me?

She said, "I . . ., I don't know."

"Does he love you?"

"I don't know!" Lorelei snapped. "I think . . . I think he's more interested in you than in me anyway."

"No way," responded Kelsey. "He's not my type. I mean he's cute, and I like him, but he's careless."

"Well, that's how I feel."

They stared at each other for a long moment in

a standoff of emotional turmoil.

Kelsey asked, "Well, what's it going to be? Are you going to cover for him?"

The lines between right and wrong seemed to blur. Lorelei doubted that this would end well.

"No," said Lorelei, but doubt trickled through her mind. "I just have to sort out how I feel." She tried to push the thought away, feeling overwhelmed.

Was Ryan falsifying records?

CHAPTER 16

Unavoidable

"**I** don't think this was sabotage. I think it was mischief," said Gallant, sitting across from the XO in his cabin.

The thought came to him that he should be able to confide in Margret Fletcher. It was ill-considered to hesitate to be open and frank with the person who was the second-in-command of one of the most powerful ships in the fleet—one who must be ready to step into his shoes if he fell in battle. If he was sensible, he should make another attempt to win her support. He should set aside his initial impressions and apprehensions about her loyalty and judgment.

"Why would you think that Captain?" asked the XO, sitting stiff and straight-backed in her chair. She was uncomfortable with discussions in the captain's cabin.

He sat still, listening to the irony of her words.

She was entangled in her meritless investigation—content to run over anyone who interfered with her standards of order and discipline. He could not—simply would not—challenge her in so direct a way as to add fuel to her more ruthless instincts.

"Because the problem was confined to Squadron 6. Sabotage of system-wide equipment in maintenance, or crews, would be uniform across squadrons."

There that settled it, he thought. He forced himself to smile at her while withholding the fact that Kelsey had given him Ryan's logbook. That was a judgment he would be bound by. He was forced to be selective in his accommodation of her.

She furrowed her brows and leaned toward him. "Still, it would not be prudent to rule out those dangerous concerns without further investigation."

He said, "Certainly not. I leave the inquiry into sabotage in your capable hands. Let me know if you find hard evidence to act upon."

"Aye aye, sir." She left his cabin with an eager step that troubled him. It was painful to see the unbounded happiness with which she set out.

Gallant turned his attention to the pilots and his more realistic assessment of the problem. The officers had so little free time that he was surprised to discover that several of them were reported milling about the lower decks during off-hours. There was nothing of interest for them to do there. It added to his suspicion that the logbook had ignited. He wondered if there was some pilot mischief involved.

129

Examining the ship schematics, he identified three possible locations where miscreants could get into shenanigans. One was the empty number three fuel tank. The second was the port side storage locker, which was under repair. The last possibility was the void space between the ship's hull and the lower deck compartment.

Gallant considered sending the XO to investigate these spaces.

No. I can't count on her.

He decided to investigate himself rather than make a fool of himself before the whole ship with a meritless accusation.

He went exploring a black and glassy empty fuel tank. Opening the inspection hatch was harder than he planned and required a torque wrench. When he managed to crack it open, the tank was forty degrees colder than the ship. He poked his head inside and choked from lack of oxygen. He backed out and shut the hatch.

Touching his comm badge, he asked the AI for directions to the storage locker under repair. It was on the other side of the ship and required him to walk through areas where the crew was moving equipment.

"Good day, Captain," was the standard greeting. He nodded and said, "As you were," before leaving the passageway.

When he reached the storage locker, it had the same feel as the fuel tank, a cold, hollow, fog without a breath to breathe.

Now he was more determined than ever to solve this mystery of the delinquent pilots. He set out once more to cross through some of the least-traveled spaces in the warship. He was the commanding officer of this vessel, and it was his duty to make an appropriate inquiry into the troubling accidents, even if he might appear foolish. He felt a doubt that he might blunder about the lower decks and find himself calling for help.

Touching his comm badge, he said, "Identify the nearest access hatch to the void space between the deck and the hull."

The AI rattled on about several nearby hatches followed by a list of safety regulations for the entry of void spaces.

"Enough," he said.

He walked a hundred meters to the access point. It was in the corner of two intersecting passageways flat on the deck.

He considered calling for help.

"Who would I ask?" he muttered. "What would I tell them? That I'm on a fishing expedition for guys playing hooky?"

Shaking off the impulse, he opened the hatch. When he entered the void space between the ship's lowest deck and the inner hull, he found condensate on the hull. An occasional drop of moisture fell to the deck. He ran his hand over the surface and his face contoured into a melancholy frown. He could already guess what he would find. He noted the time. A chill penetrated his thin jacket as he opened the hatch. The void compartment had good oxygen content and was as warm as the rest of the vessel. It was dark where he entered. He found a label tag that identified it as hatch HX011002456VD. He didn't recognize the information that the tag offered about this void space. It was situated close to a central elevator shaft which would make it accessible from the crew's quarters.

The space wasn't high enough to stand, so Gallant had to crouch as he wobbled forward along the area. There was no light inside the void other than the light streaming in from the open hatch. He felt embarrassed that he had failed to bring a flashlight with him for his investigation. He passed several partitions, but they were not airtight. He was about to give up when he saw a faint light twenty meters farther along the crawl space. He stopped and listened. There were indistinct sounds ahead. The farther he crawled, the more noises and shadows were evident. There had to be a more convenient entrance for whoever was using this space.

After skinning his shin, he had crawled far enough to hear voices. There was another partition separating him from the activity.

When he passed by the partition, the space grew to two-meter-high opening. He stood up and was saddened by what he discovered—a half dozen pilots.

They were arguing about who was the winner of the last card game.

Ryan was in the middle of the room, shouting something indistinct.

Gallant stepped into the light, looking bewildered. His white shirt was covered with grease and rust, and his trousers were ripped below the knees.

The men froze and became deadly quiet.

His torn, dirty, and disheveled uniform made him appear more like an apparition than their commanding officer.

Gallant said, "I'm shocked and disappointed with you," glowering at each in turn.

"What are you doing here?"

They all started talking at once, "Captain, we didn't..."

"We haven't been..."

"I assure you, Captain..."

They started to make excuses, "We're off-duty, sir."

"We're just trying to relax."

Gallant considered it a stroke of good fortune that one spoke up to defend them with such a flimsy excuse. It allowed him to react sharply. "You must be the 'sea lawyer' for the group. Are you prepared to defend these men in their Court-martial?"

The pilots took a step back.

After a moment, Ryan spoke up, "It's only a little horseplay, sir."

Gallant said, "For now, you're all on report and suspended from duty until further notice."

That shut them up.

"Me too, sir?" asked Ryan.

"You are relieved as squadron leader and confined to your quarters. Your failure here is a great disappointment to me. Now get out."

CHAPTER 17

Deployment

Alaina waited at the space station gangway, hoping Henry would keep his promise to say goodbye before the *Constellation* buttoned up for deployment.

The deployment was an ordinary ship departure—as ordinary as any ship leaving for a combat zone in time of war could be—with no fanfare, no speeches, no reporters. Only family members.

Hundreds of families surrounded Alaina, each obsessed with last-minute hugs and kisses that had to last for ... a month ... a year ... a lifetime.

One middle-aged woman, seeing Alaina searching the crowd, said, "Don't worry, dearie. He'll come. They always race around like mad at the last minute, but they never miss the last goodbye."

Alaina gave a faint smile to the woman. "Thank you. I'm sure you're right. I just wish for once he wouldn't make me wait until the very last moment."

The woman gave a harsh laugh. "I've done the tearful farewells and the joyful homecomings seven times. But this is my hardest goodbye yet. I was here to welcome him home barely three months ago and didn't expect him to be leaving again so soon. My Dave was due for discharge until they changed the enlistment period. Somehow, it doesn't seem fair."

Alaina put an arm around her shoulders and gave a squeeze. "I'm sorry."

The woman blinked back tears and pulled herself together. "Between my work and two kids in school, I just keep telling myself, 'It is what it is. It'll be all right.'"

The haunted smile on the woman's face lingered in Alaina's mind as she turned to walk away.

But a running man almost knocked Alaina over in his hurry to reach the woman. The two of them clung to each other, their goodbyes muffled through a blizzard of sobs and tears. Two little girls clutched at their father, pleading, "Don't go, Daddy. Please don't go."

The man eventually pried his daughters off his legs and gave his wife one final kiss. As he disappeared into the crowd, the woman knelt on the floor, holding her children close. Four spaghetti arms wrapped around her neck; two tear-stained faces buried themselves in her chest.

The woman whispered, "Be brave. Don't let Daddy see you cry. Be strong for him."

Seven years into a cruel war, the sacrifice of military families seemed forgotten in the rollercoaster swings between the pride of service and the sorrow of separation.

Alaina's eyes welled up as she watched this little drama repeat many times over the next hour.

Gallant was about to flee from the bridge and race to the dockside gangplank. He only had a precious few minutes left to say his goodbye.

"Captain. Captain Gallant," said the OOD. "Admiral Collingsworth is at the forward hatch, sir. He wishes to speak to you immediately."

Gallant stopped midstride, torn once more by the tension between desire and duty.

"Very well," he said, but it wouldn't be 'very well' if he failed to make his goodbyes.

Hustling to the forward hatch, he saw Collingsworth waiting impatiently.

"Ah, Gallant, I shan't keep you but a moment. I know you have a million things pulling on you just now."

Gallant tried to catch his breath.

Collingsworth had not changed since they had last met. He stood with his usual poised, proud bearing in his immaculate uniform. While he looked stern and overbearing, Gallant sympathized with the vast responsibility that weighed on his shoulders.

"Is the *Constellation* ready?" asked the old man.

In his mind's eye, Gallant could picture the interior of the *Constellation*, with every cubic meter crammed with people and equipment. It had been a Herculean accomplishment to prepare her for deployment. The ingenuity, tenacity, and backbreaking task had required every man and woman aboard to strain to their utmost to make it possible.

"Yes, sir," said Gallant.

"You have your full complement?"

"Yes, sir."

"You've installed all the essential equipment and supplies?"

"Yes, sir."

"Your shakedown issues are all resolved."

"Yes, sir."

"You passed all the proficiency exams for personnel and certifications for equipment?"

"Yes, sir."

A few minutes ago, Gallant had been grasping for the words to ease Alaina's sense of loss. Now he was searching for words to reassure his Commander-in-Chief that his professional duties had been correctly discharged.

He said, "The *Constellation* is ready in all respects to meet her combat assignment, sir."

The admiral said, "You know I wanted to command this mission. The president refused. The best I could do was to place someone I trusted in a position to make a difference."

They stared at each other for a long moment letting the full import of those words seep in.

"I'll do my best, sir."

Collingsworth stuck out his hand and said,

"Good luck, Henry. I know you won't let those Marines down."

When at last Gallant appeared, Alaina put her hands on his face, kissed him, and said simply, "Come back to me."

CHAPTER 18

Captain's Mast

Captain Henry Gallant sat behind a bulky oak desk in his elegant stateroom. Conducting Captain's Mast was one of his most distasteful duties. Today, the future of six of his fighter pilots was in the balance. A chore he wished—not at all.

Crisp in his best uniform and sitting ramrod-straight, he gazed at the accused, all standing at attention in the center of the room. A Marine guard stood beside his desk. But the more ominous presence was the indictment on the captain's desk.

Commander Fletcher had drawn up the indictment. She had vehemently recommended that the accused be held for court-martial. The paper in front of Gallant bristled with red marks and official seals.

Gallant's response to her was simple. "The United Planets needs fighting men and women. It's our job to train and lead them so they can serve. If they fail, it's as much our failure as theirs. This matter will go to Mast."

He squinted to bring the pilots into sharper focus. Despite the pressed uniforms and regulation trimmed hair, they looked anxious and uncomfortable. He hoped that having all parties present to give evidence would help reach an equitable resolution.

"At ease, gentlemen." His eyes swept down the line, and he continued in a steady, unemotional voice, "You are accused of drinking and gambling aboard the Constellation while she was conducting operations."

The pilots fidgeted and looked at one another.

"You have the right to refuse captain's mast and request a court-martial. Please step forward if you elect court-martial."

Gallant waited for a long and tense two minutes, but none of them stepped forward.

"Very well," said Gallant. "How do you plead?"

He didn't want to testify against them, so he breathed a quiet sigh of relief after each 'guilty' answer in turn.

He said, "Considering the seriousness of the charge, I am imposing the maximum penalty allowable under fleet guidelines. You will forfeit one-half of your pay for four months. You are restricted to ship limits for four months. And a reprimand will be placed in your service record."

He watched the emotions play out on the young men's faces. They wanted to protest the harsh punishment but held their tongues.

"Further, Ensign Ryan is demoted from squadron leader."

That blow hit home. Ryan looked ready to explode but steeled himself to accept the loss of rank without protest. The others looked sick as the gravity of the penalty sank in.

"Permission to speak, sir?" asked Flannery.

"Granted."

"We were recreating in our off-time, sir. We were trying to relax and build team spirit. Ryan was only with us a couple of times. When you found us, he was telling us to quit playing and get some sleep, sir."

"That's right," said another.

"So, you all feel that Ryan should remain your leader?"

"Yes, sir. He's one of the guys," came a chorus of agreement.

Gallant recognized that much of the young pilot's life journey mirrored his own. Like Ryan, he had lost his parents at an early age. He was bullied in his youth and had a contentious start to his Navy career. He acknowledged Ryan's talent, intelligence, and eagerness to serve. Yet, he was self-indulgent, selfish, and reckless—unacceptable traits in a leader.

"As your squadron leader, Ryan isn't supposed to be one of the guys. He is responsible for you, for the team," said Gallant. "He failed in that duty."

His eyes boring into Ryan, he went on, "You seem to think that all-night drinking and gambling was nothing more than good sport—that your squadron's dismal flying performance was unrelated to your own lapse in judgment."

Shamefaced, Ryan stared at the carpet, unable to meet his captain's eyes.

"Your behavior was not only juvenile but dangerous. Two pilots are in the hospital, and several crew members also suffered injuries while coming to their aid. The material damage was extensive."

Guilty looks replaced the defiance.

Gallant stood and walked around his desk. He leaned close and whispered to Ryan, "You'll never be a leader until you can put the welfare of your people above your own interests and ambitions."

CHAPTER 19

Ross

Gallant ordered, "Helm, collapse the warp bubble."

The bridge of the *Constellation* burst into activity.

A moment later, "Warp bubble collapsed, sir."

The ripples in the space-time fabric went unnoticed as the ship dropped out of hyperspace at the farthest edge of the Ross system—three light-days from the star.

"Very well. Ahead standard."

"Aye aye, sir," said the helmsman, smoothly transferring propulsion from the dark-matter FTL engine to the sub-light antimatter reactors. At 0.1 C, they would reach Charlie in 30 days.

For some crewmen, the transition caused space sickness ranging from dizziness to nausea. Gallant noted only slight discomfort, but he watched those around him for anyone who might be unable to meet their duties.

"Flash message from the flagship, sir," reported the communications officer.

"Read it, Ensign," said Gallant.

> From: Commander 3rd Fleet
>
> To: All ships
>
> Subj: Deployment for the Ross System
>
> Ref: (a) Ops Order File 787 (b) Mission Charlie

1. Under reference (a) 3rd Fleet will assume formation Tango 7.5.1 and proceed: heading 010, up 02, speed 0.1 C.
2. Under reference (b) convoy and escort will proceed to Charlie with all dispatch.
3. UPSS *Warrior* SS 519 will conduct recon and establish outposts in the asteroid field.
4. UPSS *Glorious* CVS-646 will launch fleet CSP.
5. UPSS *Constellation* CVS-647 will launch convoy CSP and deep space recon.
6. Report all contacts to the flagship.

Simon L. Graves

Vice Admiral Simon L. Graves UPN

Commander 3rd Fleet - UPSS *Glorious* CVS-646

"Acknowledge," said Gallant.

"Aye aye, sir."

A moment later, "Acknowledgement sent to the flag, sir."

Gallant considered the orders. The convoy was directed to run to Charlie with a destroyer escort while the rest of the fleet followed. Of immediate concern to the *Constellation* were the tasks to provide fighter cover for the convoy and long-range recon for the fleet.

He was glad that the *Warrior*, with its strong stealth capabilities, would scout ahead. Carriers, dreadnaughts, and transports had only modest stealth, compared to the moderate capabilities of the rest of the fleet.

"Officer of the Deck, take station CV#4 in fleet formation Tango 7.5.1."

"Aye aye, sir," responded the OOD, and snapped out the appropriate course change orders.

As the *Constellation* took her place in the fleet formation, Gallant considered Collingsworth's last word, "I was disappointed that the president chose Admiral Graves to command of Third Fleet instead of me. The best I could do was to include the *Constellation*. I know you'll make a difference. Don't let those Marines down."

When the ship was in formation, the OOD reported, "Ship is on station, sir."

"Report to the flag," said Gallant.

"Aye aye, sir."

"Flag acknowledged, sir."

"Very well. Launch combat space patrol and deep space recon."

Crews scrambled to bring the vehicles to the catapults. With crisp precision, the *Constellation* spit ships out into the star system.

"Combat space patrol launched, sir."

"Very well."

"Recon mission launched, sir."

"Very well."

An hour later, the OOD reported, "Initial sensor scans are clear, sir."

Gallant settled into his chair for a long wait.

A few days later, the XO reported the latest status, "Captain, the convoy and their escort are now several light-hours ahead of the fleet. Our six-fighter CSP is flying cover. Squadron 10 reports reconnaissance is radiating outward. No bogies reported."

"Thank you, XO," said Gallant. "I wonder why Admiral Graves is keeping the fleet at the outer edge of the system?"

"I imagine he doesn't want to be caught by surprise," responded Fletcher blandly.

The communication officer interrupted, "Sir, a message from planet Baker reports bombing activity.

Pacing across the bridge, his head bent in concentration, Gallant muttered, "So, they've got a carrier in the system somewhere. That'll give Graves even more reason to be overcautious."

He remained on the bridge to monitor activity for several more hours before taking a rest. Immediately falling asleep, but after only a few minutes, the OOD minutes woke him with a minor report. The pattern repeated itself several times. He listened to each report without reproach, but eventually, convinced he would get no sleep, he sat up and swung his legs off the bed. A splash of water on his face, and a few minutes later, he was back on the bridge.

The OOD said, "Good day, sir."

Gallant gave a tired nod and punched in a request for coffee. After a few gulps, his mood brightened.

The communication officer reported, "Message from the flag, sir. 'All ships maintain proper station.'"

Gallant was surprised by the subtle rebuke. Minor course adjustments were handled by AI. When errors crept into the trajectory, a human correction was necessary. He examined the sensor log and plot. The fleet had not only fallen farther behind the convoy, but a recent course change pointed them toward Baker.

"Why are we so far behind the convoy?" he asked the OOD.

"The flag keeps reducing fleet speed, sir."

"Yes, but why?"

"The flag hasn't explained, but it has also ordered the convoy to accelerate."

Later that day, Ensign Edward Decatur reported, "*Constellation,* this is Squadron 6 Leader flying convoy cover. A Titan reconnaissance ship was spotted in the vicinity of the convoy. Pursuit has been initiated."

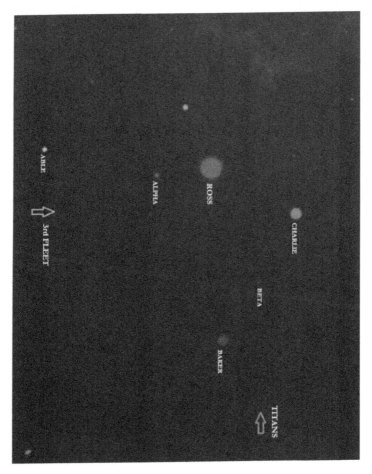

Figure 2: The *Constellation* dropped out of warp at the farthest edge of the Ross star system three light-days from the sun (relative bearing 010). Planet Able was less than one light-day away to port (relative bearing 300). Planet Baker was four light-days away to straight ahead (relative bearing 000).

In the Ross Star System

3rd Fleet – Vice Admiral Simon L. Graves - Rear Admiral Benjamin Buford Butler

> 4 Dreadnought –
> *Vanguard, Valiant, Vanguard, Victory*
> 4 Battlecruisers –
> *Redoubt, Renown, Repulse, Respite*
> 4 Spacecraft Carriers –
> *Constellation, Courageous, Glorious, Saratoga*
> 24 Cruisers
> 48 Destroyers
> 48 Auxiliary Support Ships
> Stealth Recon – *Warrior*

CHAPTER 20

Ace

"Lucky, pursue and destroy Tango one."

"Roger, squadron leader," said Ryan, grinning to himself.

It's going to be a fantastic day!

He increased his oxygen flow and breathed deeply. The air seemed different somehow—cleaner, freer, better than the stale, recycled air of the *Constellation*.

The Titan ship blipped onto his screen and then disappeared. It had a stealth rating of seven, so he only caught a glimpse, but it was enough to lay in an intercept course.

He shoved his stick hard over, the Viper hissing as it accelerated in pursuit. He found his rhythm and felt the adrenaline rush of the spine-chilling speed. The heading took him through a thin asteroid field.

Tango one had a considerable lead, but the

recon ship was built for distance, not speed. The Viper's powerful engines would apply all the acceleration needed to close the gap.

A cluster of asteroids loomed ahead. Ryan shifted to go around. The edges of his ship biting hard into the turn and swung past the first clump of rocks. He straightened up and turned to avoid several other obstacles. Then he maneuvered through a series of dust clouds, carving an extended S-shape.

He was delighted with the performance of the Viper. Another glimpse of the target told him, he was closing in.

He aimed his ship straight down a path between rocks and felt the joy of zooming along a gap. The thrill of speed and mastery over the asteroid terrain far outweighed any concern of danger.

After a minute, he glanced at his scanner. There was no sign of Tango one. A momentary concern flashed through his mind, but a moment later, he caught another glimpse.

He swung back and zig-zagged through the asteroids, driving his ship in hard.

Tango one managed to stay ahead of him by tracing a cleaner path through the field.

Ryan scolded himself for his sloppy flying.

Keep forward. Keep your focus.

Staying in Tango one's track, he closed the distance. He pushed hard, trying to catch up, straining on each turn.

Another glimpse told him that the enemy had radically altered course. A moment later, he understood why. Three Titan fighters were coming to the recon ship's rescue.

Three was too many.

A touch of fear registered. It wasn't possible that he doubted his courage, but ...

Recklessness had its limits, he knew. He treated every new challenge like the first—an opportunity to rediscover his courage. The momentary impulse to turn and run vanished. Instead, he aimed his ship's nose directly at the enemy and charged ahead, maximum thrust.

He had something to prove.

He took in a deep breath and buried his concern. Pointing his ship at the enemy, he pushed the lever to maximum thrust.

Over tac 1 he reported, "I have three new contacts, Tango two, three, and four. Fighters. Will engage."

He knew it would take several minutes for his squadron leader, Edward Decatur, to receive the message. By then, it would all be over—one way or another.

The three fighters were on an intercept course which suited Ryan just fine. Their stealth rating was a five, so he was able to track them better as the range closed. They flew in a vee formation, and as they approached, he saw the recon ship receding.

Too bad, but I have other things to think about now.

He considered the Titan ships, trying to gauge their strengths and weaknesses. Their power profile was not very different from his ship.

"AI, what are the Titan fighter's vulnerabilities."

The Viper's video console displayed the skeleton of a ship with several color-coded lines. The sensor blind spots and force shield low energy points were highlighted. Both pieces of information were welcome. He could maneuver to minimize his visibility and aim his weapons to hit precisely where the enemy would feel it.

But even with that information he still needed to account for the individual pilots in the Titan crafts. Were they top gun pilots? Or raw recruits?

He would soon find out.

The asteroid field was becoming thicker, and Ryan had to maneuver to avoid a massive asteroid as it blurred into an impenetrable wall. The sun glistened off its surface, a sharp stretch of rock with dark shadows obscured its terrain. A flurry of smaller orbiting rocks surrounded it. Finally, he saw an opening and shot past the obstacle.

As he straightened his course, the trio of fighters came in for a strafing run.

The first exchange of fire scored no hits on either side. They were moving too fast at each other.

As Ryan turned sharply to starboard, he saw the Titans break formation to chase him.

Tango two's turn brought it a few scant seconds in front of him. Ryan launched a missile at point-blank range that found its target.

Tango two exploded.

Ryan was giddy, and only the appearance of

Tango three and four converging on him shocked him back to reality.

He was a sitting duck. A lump formed in his throat.

They'll be in range in seconds.

Throwing caution to the wind, he did the only thing he could think of—he accelerated toward the fighters.

Immediately, the aliens fired two missiles.

He released decoys and fired two antimissiles. The AMM-5 Mongooses flushed from their racks. Within seconds, they locked on to their target and tracked them through a sophisticated algorithm based on emissions data, direction, and velocity.

As the Titan missiles raced toward him, Ryan felt his AI system working to home in on the target. He followed the Mongoose flight path with his mind.

One enemy missile exploded.

Too close.

His ship twisted and leaped in response to his thoughts, but he didn't dare take his eyes off the asteroids ahead.

The other missile exploded behind him with a blinding flash of light.

He found himself in the asteroid field's densest area. He cursed as he wrenched past a rock. His survival instincts took over. He quickened the pace. A dozen potential escape paths flew through his mind —each as unworkable as the next. As he followed the curve of the field to port, he came upon another row of obstructions. The trajectory of several large boulders rose up before him.

The asteroid density eased a bit. The dust sprayed out from the abrupt turn crystallized for a moment. It was all black in the distance.

He closed in on Tango three as she ran an S-turn through the field.

Ryan's head throbbed, and his muscles ached from a combination of exertion and dehydration. His joints ground and creaked. His fingers refused to release their grip. But before the enemy fighter could fire another missile, he launched his.

Tango three exploded.

Now it was one-on-one. He swung his ship hard to port and accelerated, wondering where Tango four was.

Without warning, his ship caught an edge of a small meteor and began to gyrate wildly. His breathing became labored. He was sweating profusely. Every sense turned against him as he struggled to regain control.

After a frightful few minutes, he had control and leveled off.

With an effort, he pulled off his gloves and unzipped his flight jacket. Cradling his stiff hands to his chest, he felt like a drowning man trying to catch his breath.

As he frantically looked for Tango four, he thought...

Is he that good?

The next few minutes were a blur as he operated more on instinct than reason. His opponent was the best he ever faced. He maneuvered through the asteroids with precision and at moments, brilliance.

Then the AI blared, ALERT! ZERO BEARING RATE WITH TARGET!

He was out of time, and he had so much to do—or rather, just one thing.

Survive.

He wrenched the Viper into a bone-crushing turn and fired his last missile.

Before his lips could move in silent prayer, he felt the shock wave and the explosion filled his viewscreen.

Did I win?

Ryan walked into the ready room and saw Lorelei hunched over her tablet.

She threw him a glance but turned away as soon as he opened his mouth.

Stung, he asked, "Aren't you going to congratulate me?"

Lorelei stared into his dark eyes but said nothing.

After a moment, he said, "This mission brings my career confirmed kills to five."

"You're an ace?"

"Yeah."

"Congratulations," she said quietly.

Puffing out his chest, Ryan said, "This means the captain will have to reinstate me as squadron leader."

She shook her head. "I'm afraid not."

"Why not? I'm the only ace on this ship."

"Captain Gallant is an ace many times over."

"That doesn't count. He's not flying anymore," growled Ryan. "Besides, why shouldn't he make me squadron leader?"

Lorelei sighed. "You don't get it, do you?"

"Get what?"

"There's more to being a leader than just flying. Or even combat."

Ryan ground his teeth, his eyes blazing. He pointed an accusing finger and said, "You were the one who turned my logbook in for captain's mast."

"No!"

Then she added meekly, "Well, not exactly."

"Then how exactly?"

"I confided in someone who turned it in."

He scowled.

"It was the right thing to do. I should have done it myself," she said.

"How can do you blame me for those accidents?"

"I don't blame anyone for the accidents. They're called accidents because they're no one's fault. But can you stand there and tell me you don't bear any responsibility? That you didn't do anything wrong?"

Ryan dropped his eyes and swallowed hard. "I didn't enter the accident data because I wanted to investigate first. Gallant wasn't fair. Playing cards and having a few drinks with my squadron was a way to build camaraderie with the team. I didn't think it would cause any problems."

Her face mirrored her disappointment. "Drinking and gambling with your team until all hours. Not getting enough sleep and reporting for duty with legendary hangovers. You didn't think that would lead to accidents?"

His face twisted in anger, and he turned to walk away.

She grabbed his arm. "Lucky, don't you realize what you did? The position you put me in?"

His look softened as his heart sank. "I never meant to involve you."

"But you did. I was ... disappointed."

For the first time, he looked in her eyes. "Sometimes, ... I disappoint myself."

CHAPTER 21

Convoy

At four bells in the morning watch, several CIC analysists crowded onto the bridge of the *Constellation* and rushed to Gallant's side. He was surprised to receive several reports all at once.

The OOD reported, "Sir, we've received an urgent report from the *Warrior*."

Gallant shook his head—urgent messages were never good news. "Read it aloud."

"Many Titan ships spotted near Baker including one spacecraft carrier."

The OOD said, "Captain, there are more reports of enemy activity."

One analyst reported, "The convoy is now two light-days from Charlie."

He had barely finished when a second analyst jumped in. "One of our Hawkeyes reported a Titan cruiser-destroyer force moving to intercept the convoy. We've also glimpsed a few detections that may prove to be aberrations popping up on the outer edges of our sensors' detection range."

The first analyst added, "We may be getting glimpses of Titan stealth operations, or it might be drones."

The second analyst said, "The convoy is reporting that bombers are approaching."

Biting down a string of curses, Gallant asked, "Have there been any messages from the flagship?"

"No, sir," the three chimed together.

"OOD, send a flight of bombers to attack the Titan cruisers."

That's all I can do for now.

Gallant worked with his team to evaluate what were real concerns and what were phantoms.

A later message from the flagship ordered a course change. While the convoy and its destroyer escort would proceed to Charlie, the Third Fleet was now heading for Baker.

Gallant was dismayed. Was the flagship misinterpreting the reports and heading in the wrong direction?

Several hours later, Ryan led twelve fighters as CSP leader to protect the convoy.

Twenty-four bombers attacked in vee formation. The convoy ships took evasive action, and their destroyer escorts opened fire.

Ryan scanned the battlefield through his neural

interface. The ships' positions unfolded in his mind. In a flash of insight, he considered a risky move. He split his force into two groups to simulate a hammer and anvil attack on the Titan bombers.

"Fighter flight one remain on the sunward side of the convoy. Flight two follow me around the convoy."

As he led flight two toward the Titans' flank, he snapped out orders to assign targets.

A minute later, he ordered, "Fire missiles!"

The Titans responded with decoys and electronic jamming. But the missiles were effective against the bomber formation.

"Save some for us," yelled Bear from flight one.

Ryan grinned.

The bombers returned fire, and an explosion rocked Ryan's Viper. He struggled to maintain his focus. He dove to avoid further shock waves from the thermal blast. The ship screamed in protest at the erratic maneuver, and he wondered whether it would take the strain. A small internal fire sprang up in his cockpit.

He took stock of the ship's condition. His fighter threw out smoke belching from his console. A second explosion snapped his head back against the seat. He slumped forward, unconscious for several seconds. He couldn't make sense of anything over the confusion that churned in his head.

The demand to keep his fighters engaged was taxing under his present condition. He ordered, "Break into pairs. Independent action."

The remaining Titan bombers launched a missile barrage at the transports. The missiles proved powerful against the thin-skinned auxiliary ships. The *Mims* dropped out of formation. The convoy commander's ship, *Nemo*, was damaged moments later.

The dogfight lasted several more minutes, and a dozen Titan bombers were destroyed. Finally, the bombers withdrew.

The convoy slowed to regroup.

An hour later, the Titan force of several cruisers and destroyers approached the convoy.

The convoy commander reported, "Enemy in sight."

The Titans attacked the convoy escorts and exchanged missiles.

The *Constellation's* bombers arrived in time to attack the cruisers. Lorelei led twelve bombers in an attack on the lead cruiser.

She was pressed back into her seat as she turned hard after she launched a missile barrage.

A moment later a cruiser exploded in a massive fireball.

The action continued to unfold as the convoy maneuvered frantically to dodge enemy missiles. Several convoy transports suffered hits, but none proved fatal.

Over the next twenty minutes, Lorelei's bombers succeeded in destroying two cruisers and damaged two others. The Titan ships were forced to retreat.

As the convoy regrouped and rescued survivors, Gallant was surprised to receive new orders.

CHAPTER 22

Spec Ops

From: Commander 3rd Fleet
To: Commodore Gallant, UPSS *Constellation* CVS-647
Subj: Formation of Task Force 34
Ref: (a) Ops Order File 787 (b) TF 34 Ships (c) Mission Charlie (d) Spec. Ops.

1. Under references (a) and (b) you will assemble and assume command of Task Force 34.
2. You will continue to provide cover for the relief convoy per reference (c)
3. Under reference (d) you will proceed to outpost Alpha and conduct special reconnaissance operations.

Simon L. Graves

Vice Admiral Simon L. Graves UPN
Commander 3rd Fleet - UPSS *Glorious* CVS-646

Reference (b): **Task Force 34** – Commodore Henry Gallant

1 Spacecraft carrier – *Constellation*
2 Battlecruisers –
Indefatigable, Indomitable
6 Cruisers
18 Destroyers
1 Stealth Recon - *Warrior*

Gallant's first reaction was a rush of pride at the new title. Then his command response kicked in.

The Marine battalion on Baker was under attack by one carrier and an assault convoy. Graves was leading the Third Fleet to engage the Titan landing force and wanted Gallant's task force to protect the relief convoy on its way to Charlie. Task Force 34 would also conduct recon operations to uncover any other hidden Titan ships.

The bridge was where Gallant faced his toughest decisions, where he found the most satisfaction, where he felt most alive. He leaned back in his captain's chair and looked around, mentally analyzing the surprising orders.

Could the attack on Baker be a diversion?

In that case, the Third Fleet should stay together to relieve the larger Marine force on Charlie.

He sent a message to the flagship suggesting the

possibility and his analysis of the strategic situation.

Graves' reply came back promptly: "Follow your orders."

Gallant stuck his hand out. "Welcome aboard, John."

"I'm glad to see you again, Commodore," said Roberts, pumping Gallant's hand, his face beaming. "I never thanked you for standing up for me at the debriefing."

"Not necessary."

"Thank you anyway," said Roberts. He handed across a bottle of fine Scotch.

Surprised at the gesture, Gallant said, "'I'll keep this for a special occasion."

"How do you like the *Constellation*?"

Now it was Gallant's turn to grin. He swung his arm in a wide arc to encompass not just the elegant stateroom, but the entire ship. "She's everything I could have asked for."

A rap at the door interrupted them. A Marine stepped inside and announced, "Officers are ready to make their reports, Commodore."

"Let them in."

Fletcher, the squadron leaders, and several other officers filed into the stateroom.

Gallant gestured for them to be seated. "I've asked you here to discuss the upcoming special operations we are to conduct with the *Warrior*. This is

Captain John Roberts. Ready, John?"

Roberts said, "A week ago, the *Warrior* established a charging base in the asteroid belt, designated outpost Alpha. From there, we've scouted the central region of the star system. We got a glimpse of a carrier and a convoy near Baker a couple of days before they attacked the planet."

Heads nodded around the room.

He continued, "The Titans have been in this system for a while but only recently started building a base on Charlie. That was what the Second Marines took from them. And now they're trying to take it back. No doubt they're scrambling to reinforce their forward bases, and this is a key point. Now Admiral Graves has redirected the Third Fleet toward Baker, leaving TF34 to escort the relief convoy to Charlie."

Gallant scowled. "The Marines have a reputation for never backing down. We will support them."

"That's why I'd like to establish a second outpost on the far side of the asteroid field to observe enemy movements," said Roberts. "From outpost Beta, the *Warrior* will be able to observe the entire far side of the Ross system."

The XO asked, "What do you need from *Constellation*?"

"If TF34 will send a shuttle with my men and equipment, they can find the best location for the base and get it set up before the *Warrior* arrives."

Edward Decatur, Squadron 6 leader, said, "You'll need a fighter escort."

"And a couple of Hawkeyes," added Kelsey.

"Agreed."

Gallant said, "XO, make that so. But before we disperse, I want to discuss the new alien species discovered in this system several months ago."

Roberts said, "We collected a lot of info about a battle in this system that apparently occurred several decades ago. The debris looked like the remains of a large warship and several smaller ones. We also found communications gear and picked up some automatic transmissions that we haven't been able to translate yet. I turned over all our data and artifacts to the SIA."

"No conclusions so far?" asked an officer.

Roberts said, "Not yet, but in the last week, the *Warrior* found more evidence."

"Evidence?"

"You are aware that we identified ruins on Able and Baker? We have reason to believe that plasma weapon technology from these aliens is starting to show up in Titan ships. Technology which they hadn't had before."

"Couldn't the Titans have developed it on their own?"

"Possibly, but we should have seen precursor technology if that was the case. This appeared fully developed. Intelligence intercepts indicate that the Titans are concerned about the far side of their space. Areas we've never visited."

The XO asked, "Intercepts? We don't have confidence in our ability to read the Titan language."

Gallant said, "True, but I've reviewed the material, and it appears genuine."

Silence descended as the group considered both the possibilities and the implications.

"Are the other aliens helping the Titans?" asked someone.

Roberts shook his head. "We don't think so. Based on the ruined outpost and old battle debris we found, it makes more sense that they are, or at least were, at war."

"At war? Before our war started or after?"

"No way to know," said Roberts. "The Titans seem to have been at war with them for a long time. Our best guess is that they felt we were an easy mark, a quick way to expand their buffer zone, but when we proved tougher than they expected, and they ended up in a two-front war. We may be able to use that to our advantage."

"If that's true, we should contact this other race and unite against our common foe," said another officer.

"How do we know that the others aren't worse than the Titans?" asked yet another. "Maybe the Titans were forced to fight them and then turned against us in desperation."

"That doesn't make sense. If they were already struggling, why would they take on another enemy?"

"What else do we know?" asked Gallant, raising his voice above the hubbub.

"Nothing. Only guesses at this point."

"The Titans must know lots about the other race. Why can't we infiltrate their databases and find out?"

Gallant said, "Efforts are underway to do that. The Titans don't make much information available to the public, only to the top command levels."

"How can we possibly figure out what they're thinking? We've been fighting the Titans for years, and we still have only a vague idea of how they think."

"You think this new alien species may have superior technology?" asked an officer.

"Only in a few aspects. Our investigation suggests they are inferior in other areas. But we gather that there seemed to be a balance of power between Titans and the others, and somehow we upset that balance."

Gallant considered the human-occupied worlds and stars of the human territory in comparison to the Titan area.

What does each region look like? How extensive is the Titans' reach?

"Any idea which are their stars?"

"No, but we could send ships to explore," said Roberts.

Gallant looked around the room. "The Titans like to trick us. We know they are highly intelligent, adaptable, and politically astute. Not to mention subtle. We have evidence that suggests they are manipulating us into working against our own interests. They may have found a way to influence our internal politics."

One officer said, "How could they do that? They've had no direct contact with us."

"They don't have to. They can plant messages in our communications, corrupt our AI systems. They could infiltrate our news media to spread misinformation."

"They would get caught."

"Maybe. Their survival as a species is at stake, and that means they're desperate," said Gallant. He picked up a tablet. "I have copies of the data and several artifacts that were collected. Our communications officer has examined them. Will you give a rundown of the findings, Mr. Logan?"

Logan popped up, as eager as a jack-in-a-box and let loose a flood of excited chatter.

The XO said, "Stop! I can't understand a single word you're saying. You need to slow down."

Logan froze, startled. He blushed and fumbled with his tablet.

Gallant glared at the XO. He looked at the young man and said, "Take a deep breath, Mr. Logan. Just take your time and start again."

"Yes, sir. The Chameleon were the original inhabitants of this system."

The XO interrupted, "Chameleon? I wasn't aware of that name."

Logan glanced around the room, again unsure of himself. He said, "I call them that because they have incredible stealth technology and seem to be secretive and adaptable."

"We'll keep the Chameleon designation for now. Continue," said Gallant, suppressing a smile.

"They are originally from another area of space

and colonized this system. From the remains of their dead, we found that the aliens have chips implanted in their brains. As yet, however, we know little about their motives or capabilities."

One officer asked, "That was the situation we had several years ago when we faced the Titans. Are we now facing a new enemy, or is it possible we could find them to be an ally?"

Gallant said, "That's what we're trying to determine. Mr. Logan, the *Warrior* has found new Chameleon artifacts on Able. I want you to take charge of analyzing them along with the SIA data and see what you can make of it."

Logan's eyes lit up. "Aye aye, sir!"

Ryan scrambled into his cockpit and waited his turn to launch. As the cable smoked out, the toe link shot the Viper shot into space like a pellet in a slingshot. He formed up as Decatur's wingman. They were the escort for Kelsey's Hawkeye and a shuttle jammed with equipment. They headed toward the edge of the asteroid field. The Hawkeye worked with the shuttle CIC team to check a location for outpost Beta.

Scoping the area ahead with her Hawkeye's sensors, Kelsey reported over tac1, "Rock cluster on the port beam."

"Excellent," said Decatur. "Lucky, buzz over to them and take a closer look. We'll maintain his heading."

"Will do, Hotshot," said Ryan. He pushed the throttle forward and started accelerating.

After a few minutes, Ryan said, "I've conducted a close scan and uploaded the data for CIC to evaluate."

"Good," said Hotshot, "Return to the formation."

"Will do."

The CIC analysts reported, "There isn't an asteroid large enough in that cluster. We need to keep looking."

Kelsey said, "There is a promising cluster ahead to starboard. I'll send the coordinates."

Decatur said, "Check that out, Lucky."

Once more, Ryan shot ahead and scanned the formation. He passed through a large dust cloud and had to duck many meteors. He weaved through the asteroid field as if he were playing a game, but soon he found the cluster they were interested in. He ran a series of scans and sent the data to the shuttle. This time the CIC analysts were pleased.

"There is a large central rock that we can use," said an analyst, identifying an asteroid in the cluster. The asteroid was an irregularly shaped rocky body. A special operations team deployed to the rock. They installed a power plant and a communication relay station. A satellite was placed in orbit with a focused laser transmission beam.

Later that day Decatur reported to *Constellation*, "Outpost Beta is up and running, sir. Ready for the *Warrior*."

The *Warrior* began reconnaissance operations of the far side of the star system. It wasn't long before Roberts reported disturbing sightings.

CHAPTER 23

A Grave Mistake

Vice-Admiral Simon L. Graves stood up, leaving a deep indentation on the overstuffed chair in the stylish stateroom aboard his flagship the Glorious. He wiped the sweat from his bushy eyebrows and twitchy jowls with a limp handkerchief. He stuck out his jaw and scowled. "Are you questioning my judgment?"

"Nonononono," stuttered his chief of staff, Captain Agatha Turnbull. "Not at all, Admiral. I only wanted to understand your thinking, so I can draft the action orders." Her heartbeat accelerated, and she clasped her hands to stop the trembling.

"The Marines on Baker report that Titan assault ships have started landing troops there. The Titans have one carrier, two dreadnaughts and some escorts in close orbit. The situation is so crystal clear a child could propose the perfect strategy."

Graves spread his arms, satisfied that nothing

more needed to be said.

Dismayed, Turnbull asked, "I . . . I'm sorry, sir, but can you elaborate?"

His frown deepened. "I've dispatched Collingsworth's lapdog to escort the convoy to Charlie. I'm relieved to have him out of my hair, at least for the moment. In the meantime, I will lead the Third Fleet to Baker and wipe out the Titan fleet."

"Sir, Captain Gallant has reported several large Titan formations in the vicinity of outpost Beta, heading toward Charlie."

"Nonsense."

"But sir, if Titan forces are there, we'll be too far away to intervene."

"Hogwash! He's an unreliable freak who exaggerates and inflates everything to make himself appear important. There may be a half dozen destroyers and cruisers roaming the system. They're raiders designed to stir up trouble. They may confuse the genetically inferior, like Gallant, but the Titan fleet is at Baker, and I will annihilate it in five days."

"Even so, sir, the force at Baker is powerful."

"The Third Fleet has three times its strength. We will overwhelm them and liberate the Ross System."

"You mean once Task Force 34 relieves Charlie, sir?"

"Of course. Once I defeat the Titan fleet at Baker, Charlie will be 'a walk in the park.'"

For five days, the Marines screamed for help as Graves sat comfortably on the bridge as *Glorious* cruised toward Baker. Once the Third Fleet was finally in range, he ordered, "I want a full sensor sweep. What have we got on tactical?"

"We have several distant contacts, but at this distance, stealth technology limits ship identification, sir."

Graves said, "Dispatch drones and have a few Hawkeyes take a look."

The first sighting was made later that day by the *Glorious'* Hawkeye patrol. They identified an assault convoy in orbit over the planet.

Graves decided to launch an all-out strike by two of his carriers. The *Glorious* space-wing, He held in reserve.

No sooner had the strike been launched then another sighting was reported. A carrier and two battlecruisers were located several light-minutes from Baker giving Graves a dilemma of which target to concentrate on. He ordered the strike force split in two. The *Courageous'* squadrons were to attack the landing forces while the *Saratoga's* were ordered to attack the Titan carrier.

The starfighters met the Titan fighter defenses at Baker. At first, the battle seemed well-matched, until a squadron of bombers broke into the clear and made a missile run at the transports. The lightly armored ships scattered their orbits to evade the rockets, throwing out decoys and jamming devices.

Busy defending the transports, the Titans were

left with too few fighters to protect their carrier. When the attack wave from the *Saratoga* arrived, the Titan carrier quickly suffered significant damage, though not before she managed to launch a counter-attack against the *Glorious*.

Graves was upset at the sight of incoming Titan bombers. The *Glorious* evaded the first attack, but a second flight upped the assault. Missiles launched at both port and starboard sides forced her into radical evasive action. Between her erratic movements and her screening ships, which kept up daunting flak, the carrier remained safe.

In the fray, a few bombers got through the defenses and scored a hit on a battlecruiser, but overall Graves was pleased with his handling of the battle. He had destroyed one Titan carrier and a dozen escort vessels, along with scores of auxiliary ships. The Marines on Baker were relieved as reinforcements landed and rounded up the Titan ground troops. However, two Titan battlecruisers and several escort ships escaped.

Graves turned to Turnbull and ordered, "Send a courier ship to Earth with a full report immediately. Inform UP Command of this magnificent victory that secured the Ross star system. I will include an endorsement of presidential candidate Gerome Neumann. I'm sure my name will carry significant weight when news of my success is circulated."

"Aye aye, sir," said Turnbull. "Shall I prepare to move the Third Fleet to Charlie as soon as we're satisfied Baker is secured?"

"There's no hurry to leave Baker. We need to rest the fleet and consolidate our position here. Collect any salvageable material from the destroyed and damaged Titan ships as well. They may have some intelligence value. Besides, I'd like some trophies to take home with me from this great triumph."

"But what about Charlie, sir? The Marines are still engaged, and there are sightings of enemy ships."

"I already told you to disregard those sightings. In fact, disregard anything Gallant tells you. Once the convoy reaches Charlie, all operations in Ross will cease. There's nothing left to do."

CHAPTER 24

How Heroes Die

"They've ... landed!" shouted Steward as he rushed into the midst of the bustling crowd at Marine headquarters.

'Bulldog' McIntyre chewed his wad of tobacco into a ripe gooey mass. Then he spat on the ground and wiped his mouth.

Steward said, "They have several landing zones in the mountain range surrounding the base. They're in armored methane suits, several thousand strong with heavy weapons including tanks. Another unit hit our space station."

McIntyre's voice was calm and reassuring. "We've made our preparations."

The Marine regiments (2nd, 4th, 6th, 8th) were positioned like the four points of a compass around headquarters.

Steward said, "The Titans are massing in two

large groups. One to the west and another to the east of the lava ravine."

"We can expect a two-pronged attack before dawn," said the general. He turned to Colonel Rebecca Tilden, Eighth Regiment. "Rebecca, you will defend the west."

She said, "My people have mostly light weapons and a few tanks. That's not a lot of firepower compared to what the Titans will send against us."

"Keep within your bunker system. Remember, they're fighting on orders. We're fighting for our lives. I'm depending on you to hold the west."

"You can count on my people," replied Tilden with a salute.

Placing his hand on her shoulder, the general said, "I know I can."

McIntyre turned to Steward and looked him in the eyes. He touched his arm and said, "Get to the east ravine. Don't let them cross!"

Steward flinched.

The general said, "There's less cover to the east, and the bunkers are weak where the ravine runs between them. You'll have to move your men around to hold out against the assault. Do you understand?"

"Yes, General."

"You'll have what remains of the Fourth Regiment, elements of the Tenth Tank Battalion, and what's left of the Twelfth Artillery Battalion. The last space bombardment walloped those units. You're the remaining senior officer."

McIntyre squeezed Steward's arm. "You have

the same weapons shortcomings as Rebecca, but you'll need to be more selective about where you place them. They must maintain overlapping fire and cover the more vulnerable positions. I'm counting on you to keep your wits and respond to fluctuating conditions. Can you do that?"

Steward nodded, his mind already racing through deployment options.

The general said, "Hold," through gritted teeth.

"Will do . . . General," replied Steward, wondering how he would keep that promise.

McIntyre said, "I'll remain in headquarters with our reserve. I'll deploy them as the battle progresses. Headquarters will serve as our field hospital."

"Believe me," he added, "we *will* see a better tomorrow. Now go to your positions."

Steward left and hustled through the underground tunnels, side-stepping around the barricades.

When he reached Twelfth Recon Company, he found Master Sergeant "Pappy" Papias in a dugout with his men, cleaning their guns. Steward heard them talking as he approached and paused to listen.

"This planet is a dump," he was surprised to hear Pappy say.

"Yeah," said Sonny. "I only care about my bed and my next meal, but even I can't wait to get outta this hole."

"I haven't cared about anything but my men since before you were born, Sonny. And lemme tell ya, it feels great—to not give a damn."

There were a few chuckles.

But sweat dripped down onto Sonny's helmet. The youngest member of the squad, until now he had only known war from videos. He averted his eyes and wiped a sleeve across his forehead. He asked, "Why do they call you Pappy? You're not so old."

Pappy laughed. "I'm 38, which ain't young for a Marine. But they call me Pappy because I have seven children. The youngest is Ellen, two and as ornery a new recruit as you'll ever meet." His voice swelled with pride. "She'll make a great Marine someday."

"Pappy, why are you a Marine?"

"Look, it's not easy to explain. I'm not sure it even makes sense. There are just some things that I believe. Some things that I'm willing to fight for. Wearing this uniform . . ., well, it's part of me. Like an arm or a leg."

"Ahh," muttered Sonny. "*What* are you willing to fight for?"

"That's easy. I fight for those I care about."

"How have you managed to survive so long?"

Pappy leaned back and furrowed his brow. "To survive, you must revise and adapt to find a better outcome. It's called threat assessment."

Sonny asked, "So, you would never give up?"

Pappy said, "Me? I don't believe in giving up."

"Oh, come on—that 'never give up, never surrender' stuff—doesn't there come a point when it's too hard to go on?"

"For some," said Pappy, chewing on a wad of tobacco. "But there are those who can dig deep and find something more. They carry on."

"Do you believe in luck, Pappy."

"No. Luck dies over time."

"I'd hate to die on this rock," muttered Sonny.

Pappy said, "We're all gonna die—eventually. But Marines don't lose heart."

"Never?"

"There are always *choices*. Some decide to take as many of the enemy with them in a hell-bent-for-leather charge," said the older soldier. "Others choose to hunker down and play sniper until the end. It varies."

Steward interrupted the conversation then, his voice hoarse. "Listen up, men." He cleared his throat and forced the words to snap. "We've got five klicks between here and the outer perimeter bunker. Let's move."

As the men leaped to their feet and scurried to obey, Sonny asked, "Why are we always the tip of the spear?"

Pappy snapped out orders. "When we exit the tunnels, get into ground convoy formation and move along the edge of the foothills. We have to reach the outpost fortifications."

A small Marine named Joe said, "The heavy armor won't do us a lick of good if we get hit from above."

His battle-armor rattled as he moved.

"And I'll bet this is the last of the rations for this mission," he said, grabbing an extra energy bar.

They marched. The wind picked up and blew grit at them, stinging in the thin atmosphere. They were used to the routine, but ready for conditions to go sideways at any time.

When they reached the blast-damaged fortifications on the eastern front, Steward asked, "Lieutenant Jessup, what's your status?"

The Fourth Regiment's last officer said, "The men are in position, per your instructions, sir. Two-thirds are the first line of defense, in two-man fox-holes along the ravine edge. The rest are behind, protected by a stone wall. I distributed our heavy guns to key bunkers. Our tanks are behind the hill, ready for a counterattack."

Together Steward and Jessup visited each fox-hole in turn.

Finally, Steward said, "I'll join the first line of defense. You direct the second. If we need to pull back, we'll fill in behind the stone wall."

The lieutenant nodded, her face drawn and tense.

"Listen for my signals."

She pressed her lips together and nodded once more.

He left her standing and went to the ravine without another word.

Next came the waiting. Waiting was always the worst. Stewards pulse quickened, his heart raced, and sweat formed on his brow.

As the first gray light flickered on the horizon, sounds and moving shadows started to emerge out of the darkness. Steward licked his dry lips. His eyes darted around, taking in the shadowy figures in the distance, and the dust drifting like mist in the gusting wind. His mind ran back through his placements, searching for weakness . . . but it no longer mattered. They were where they were

No time to change now.

Every sound, every shadow heightened his imagination.

Pappy appeared beside him. They faced each other for a long moment, each recognizing and acknowledging what the other knew and felt. Finally, the sergeant gestured, a slight wave of his hand. He moved like a shadow to one side and disappeared.

The next instant the early morning shattered into a firestorm over the eastern defenses as the Titans hit the first tripwire and set off the mines.

Steward's long-range search cam went black.

Dat-dat-dat-dat-dat-dat-dat-dat-dat-dat!

A spray of light machine gun fire pounded to his left. The air was thick with blaster fire.

A row of Titans appeared on the ridgeline.

Pappy shouted, "Here they come!"

Steward switched to the headquarters channel and reported, "We're in contact."

Pfft! pfft! pfft!

A spray of rifle fire ricocheted in front of him.

They crouched down and scanned the landscape. The enemy was closing to a hundred meters.

Pappy pulled his trigger a few times and then moved to a new spot and fired again.

That's when more bullets started flying.

Thpff! Thpff! Thpff!

Something large and heavy disintegrated a nearby pile of volcanic rock.

Steward froze for a moment, trying to both absorb and assess the situation. He took a few deep breaths and felt a rush of adrenaline. Clarity and certainty returned.

The heat of the volcano's lava buffeted his men along the ravine. A white flash momentarily blinded him. He blinked hard, trying to clear his vision even as he felt fragments—metal? rock? he wasn't sure—whistled past him. His breath came hard and fast, and he tasted blood in his mouth.

I got this.

Shouting for artillery support, he watched in dismay as the incoming Titans kept advancing despite the shells. He darted between foxholes, coordinating fire at the leading enemy elements, appalled at how many of his men were already wounded. Medics struggled to remove the injured under the heavy fire.

Enemy troops had already breached the defensive layout and were swarming through the gaps. They were well-armed and organized.

He heard shouts over the mic. The first line of defense was being overrun.

A shell exploded near Steward and shrapnel struck his shoulder, sending him spinning. He heard himself cry out but barely registered the pain. The self-sealing suit tightened and closed over the rip, and he kept running, dodging through the mayhem.

The battle surged around him, one horror after

another. As soon as he sent reinforcements to one weak point, another hole opened up in the crumbling defense. He knew they were on the edge of disaster.

Amid the ebb and flow of battle, the sheer numbers of the enemy broke down the second line of defense. With so many wounded, Steward could do nothing more.

He shouted over tac 1, "Lieutenant! Lieutenant?"

She was nowhere to be found.

He shouted to his men, "Fall back to the stonewall!"

He repeated it several times, and those that were able fell back.

Steward ran, gasping for breath.

He ordered the tanks to counterattack. The 100-ton mammoths floated three meters over the ground and packed a punch with an 88-millimeter laser cannon. They were a magnificent sight coming into the open and blasting away Titan infantry.

Within two minutes over a hundred Titan died, and the position was reversed. Titans were running, and Steward wanted to cheer.

Then the Titan's laser artillery targeted the tanks. One by one, the dozen monsters turned from killing machines into huge slags of molten metal.

The tank attack failed.

Steward got up and ran again, turning and firing at the advancing Titans.

Peering over his shoulder, he tripped and crashed to the ground.

The enemy was crossing the ravine—he had failed.

He lay still bleeding from the shrapnel wound. He gasped for another breath.

Trembling from exhaustion, he pulled himself up.

He ran.

The noise was thunderous, and a flash of light gave him a chance to get his bearings. He smelled the acrid fumes rising from the explosions, followed by smoke. Looking away, he crawled under a ridge, losing himself in the smoke and confusion.

Finally, he was able to clear his head of sensations. He had no idea where the rest of his men were; many were probably dead.

He tried to rally the men around the stone wall.

Others will join me.

The area was now a disaster zone. The enemy could take advantage of its vulnerability at any time. But the battle was not yet concluded.

After a few minutes, he reached a point where rocks converged into a funnel-like area.

This spot is defensible.

Are they coming this way?

He stood up and moved behind the position

Ever since he had started running, he had been operating on raw nerves. Now he tried to gather his thoughts and the remaining men.

Steward's one remaining hope was to give the general enough time to organize reinforcements.

Hunkered down behind the wall, he waited and

watched for the enemy's next move.

The explosions seemed to come from all directions. One earsplitting detonation knocked his small cadre to the ground.

What happened?

As he fought to shake off the concussion, acidic smoke and ash invaded his nostrils. Lungs heaved as he gasped and wheezed for air. He blinked to clear the tears that now streamed from his eyes. He patted across his chest, arms, and legs, then ran his fingers over his face and head. He was still in one piece.

Sound was the next sense to return, a dull roar punctuated by explosions that shook the ground and told him the battle was still going badly. His mind churned as his eyes tried to pierce the darkness. The thick haze of smoke must be obscuring the sun. He rallied his men and began moving again.

Keep firing.

He looked into the darkness with uncomprehending eyes. His ears told him the battle was going badly.

Steward heard Rebecca calling over tac2 for help. The 8th Regiment had fallen. The west defenses were breached!

The enemy had penetrated all the way to headquarters. There wasn't going to be any reinforcements.

Gathering Pappy and what was left of his men, he pulled back.

Several men laid down heavy covering fire

while he dragged an injured man back behind a barricade.

Steward shouting over the mic, "Gather at the rally point!"

Somehow Pappy would always materialize at his side. A few men rallied toward him.

Pappy ordered, "Joe cover the right flank. Sonny lay down covering fire."

Together they charged forward one more time, but they were insufficient to make a difference, and the return gunfire drove them back.

Weak from pain, Steward concentrated. Weapons pointed in his direction. He moved farther behind the wall before an irregular volley of fire streamed toward him. Once again, he found himself lying flat on the ground. His arms had no strength to lift him. The bloody battle continued with undisciplined surges between the dwindling numbers of combatants.

Steward fired his handgun and hit his target.

Shouts echoed from the fighting men around him.

From his position, he was able to pick off several of the more vulnerable enemy.

He was in the center of the battle with a ragged group of men. The ferocious battle was being waged as a wildly irregular series of personal combats.

He was confronted by an enemy warrior who was a foot taller and had arms and legs as wide as tree limbs. They fought hand-to-hand. Every part of his body ached, and stabbing pain ripped across his shoulders. Sharp pain, like broken glass, stung his hands. Swollen knuckles and joints were sore. The world swirled around him like a virtual merry-go-round.

Steward continued in the fiercest fighting. The flash of gunfire gave him enough warning to throw himself flat. Quickly, the wave of action washed past him, and he found several men moaning nearby on the ground. He tripped on a mutilated body whose vacant eyes stared up at him.

Steward found Pappy with Sonny and Joe by his side. Then a spray of gunfire struck the ground across their path. They fell to the ground and threw their backpacks in front of them for cover. They were caught on flat ground with minimal cover.

There was a gully a hundred meters away that could give them an escape route and salvation, but they couldn't reach it. A powerful Titan force of snipers and machine guns held the high ground and could blanket the area. They could cut them down the moment they showed their heads. Every motion was greeted by a sniper bullet. He knew that in a few more minutes the Titans would call in artillery. It was a matter of time before they would all be dead.

Cautiously Steward peered over the backpacks.
Pling! pling! pling! pling! pling!

He ducked down as bullets ricocheted around him. Sweat streamed down his face and shame engulfed him. This was his failure—all his fault. He had led his men to their doom and could do nothing to save them.

Pfft! pfft! pfft!

A racket of gunfire exploded to his right.

Over tac 1, he heard, "YAHOO!"

Pfft! pfft! pfft!

More gunfire showered past. Someone next to him jumped up despite the incoming barrage.

Pfft! pfft! pfft!

It was Pappy.

Steward could read his lips, "Semper Fi."

He gave Steward something between a wave and a salute, then turned and ran full tilt toward the Titan line without waiting for any tactical discussion or war council. Pappy was just doing his job.

Every Titan weapon was aimed at him. But Pappy ran and wove and dodged, never giving the enemy a clean shot. He looked like a star halfback slithering through the defensive line to break upfield. There was no stopping him on his run to the end zone.

The Titans couldn't get a bead on the dashing sergeant. Steward knew this was the opportunity they needed—a chance for his men to live.

He shouted over tac 1, "Everybody up! Head for the gully. Now! Move! Move! Move!"

Pappy ran toward the enemy while his Marines were running in the opposite direction.

From the corner of his eye, Steward saw Pappy pirouetting like a ballerina while bullets and laser beams blasted everything around him into nothingness.

Then the inevitable happened.

As Steward dropped into the gully, he threw one last look over his shoulder—and saw Pappy fall, a ragdoll in slow motion.

CHAPTER 25

Forward

The cabin was dark when Gallant woke, his mouth watering at the thought of fresh scrambled eggs, heaps of bacon, and buttered toast. He lay curled on his side, semi-conscious as he fantasized about a cup of real coffee. He could almost smell the aroma as he showered and dressed. That desire haunted him as he joined his officers in the wardroom.

As he ordered from the AI menu, he was determined to have a good breakfast.

He thought, *perhaps today will be different.*

The coffee, eggs, bacon, and toast were cooked to his specifications and delivered to the wardroom table. He forked the facsimile scrambled eggs into his mouth along with a slice of bacon. He washed it down with sim-coffee.

No, today was no different. The synthetic food simulated what he had asked for, but it didn't fool his taste buds.

He sighed and let his disappointment melt away amid the good-natured banter of the young men and women around the table.

After the meal, he sat motionless for several minutes, feeling the subtle vibration of ceaseless movement that connected him to the rhythms of his ship.

He considered himself a perceptive man—one who could weigh the rational exercise of military strategy against the physical courage of actual combat. He understood his own motivation to serve in the Navy, but he also acknowledged the things he disliked about the service. He was impatient with its political failings, sometimes stifled by its protocol. And the failure of some senior officers to grasp his strategic insights often disappointed him.

He mentally sorted through these conflicts, hoping for a resolution, until a message from CIC provided a welcome interruption.

XO Fletcher was already in the communications center.

"I've set up a videoconference with the *Warrior*," she said.

He nodded, settled in a chair and listened, as always mildly annoyed at the time delay that resulted from the distance between them.

The news was not good—an attack by a powerful Titan assault force on Charlie. The already beleaguered Marines were taking a shellacking.

"Captain Roberts, what have you learned?"

asked Gallant, repressing a sigh.

"Commodore, while the *Warrior* was cloaked, we observed an assault force consists of over sixty transport and supply ships unloading at Charlie. A carrier and escort ships were a few light-minutes away in orbit."

"We've got to relieve the Marines on Charlie before it's too late," said Gallant, his fingers digging into the chair's armrests.

"Commodore, we also observed a Titan fleet of four carriers and six dreadnaughts within four light-hours of Charlie. We've identified the Titan commander as Admiral Zzey in the carrier *Vampiri*."

"If Task Force 34 continues to Charlie," said the XO, "we'll run right into that fleet—hovering like a spider, but ready to leap like a tiger. We have to turn back to Able."

Gallant said, "Our orders are to protect the convoy and relieve Charlie."

"Maybe we should seek clarification from the admiral?" asked the XO.

"He has dismissed all the reports of a large Titan force near Charlie."

Roberts said, "Well, he has to believe that a major assault is underway since General McIntyre is broadcasting that in the clear."

Gallant asked, "You said that the Titan had four carriers four light-hours from Charlie. What's it doing there?"

"Heading toward Baker at 0.15 C. I think they are going to attack the third fleet."

Gallant said, "There's a lot of uncertainties about the enemy disposition and intentions. But the Titans are just as uncertain about us. What might Admiral Zzey believe?"

Roberts said, "He may think that our convoy turned back to Able after the bomber and cruiser attacks. He has no idea that Task Force 34 is escorting our convoy to Charlie. He would see his Charlie assault is going well and he has left a carrier covering force. So, he might be heading to Baker to tackle the third fleet."

Gallant said, "That could be our chance. We can approach Charlie undetected by taking an elliptical path using the sun's corona for cover. The opacity of the stellar atmosphere will help to obscure Titan sensors. This will optimize our stealth and give us a chance for a surprise attack. The convoy will remain several light-hours behind the task force."

Heads nodded in agreement.

"While the main Titan fleet moves toward Baker, we can land the 3rd Marine Division and stand by to protect it. If the main Zzey's fleet turns around to come at us, they would be between us and the third fleet. We could hit them from both ends. We have enough firepower to make the aliens regret tangling with this Task Force."

"This was Admiral Graves' plan all along," said the XO raising her arms over her head. "It's brilliant!"

Gallant looked incredulous. It was the XO's job to play the devil's advocate, but this was too much.

He said, "Only if Graves moves at top speed and supports our actions at Charlie."

Roberts said, "That's a big if."

The XO said, "There are a lot of ifs in that scenario."

Gallant said, "I've got an idea that may help confuse the Titans and give us an edge. Have Midshipman Logan report to me, immediately."

CHAPTER 26

Strike

War raged across the Ross star system. For most, the days varied from sullen and quiet to angry and loud. And for a long time, things felt unreal, like they were reliving events from archaic history. For the those aboard the *Constellation*, the war brought a separate more personal obligation to the Marines on Charlie.

Tense hours passed as Task Force 34 remained alert. The ship's company changed its eight-hour watch routine to a twelve-hour rotation. This kept more hands at weapon stations. The increased pace of activity brought a heightened sense of urgency. Although many had experienced danger before, the renewed sense of purpose boosted their resolve.

Keeping alert meant that recon craft constantly spiraled away from the ship like spokes from the hub of a wheel. The Hawkeye pilots searched the vast dark space for traces of the enemy.

As the watch changed to the night shift, an exhausted Henry Gallant marched onto the bridge. He had been continuously awake for twenty-four hours planning and inspecting preparations. His second-in-command was already explaining the upcoming operation to the OOD. It would cause significant disruption throughout the ship.

The bridge crew was accustomed to Gallant's silent presence when he was lost in thought. For the moment, he was considering the one major asset he had over the Titans—the *Warrior*—she had a stealth rating of 10 when cloaked. She had already penetrated the Titan defenses around Charlie while Task Force 34 remained outside of the enemy's sensor range. Now she was following the Titan main fleet commanded by Admiral Zzey in the carrier *Vampiri.*

The OOD interrupted his contemplation. "Sir, we've reached one light-hour from Charlie."

"Where is Zzey's fleet?" asked Gallant, his gravelly voice, hardly above a whisper.

"The *Warrior* reported that four carriers and six dreadnaughts are one light-day from Charlie heading toward Baker, sir."

"And the Third Fleet?" Gallant sounded as if he had marbles in his mouth.

"Third Fleet has secured Baker and is moving toward Charlie."

Even in his groggy state, Gallant was able to do the math. The third fleet would take twenty days to reach Charlie at 0.1C. The Titan main fleet could double back to Charlie in five days if they hurried at

0.2 C.

"Our relief convoy is one light-hour behind us," said the OOD. "Request permission to conduct a long-range scan of Charlie, sir."

"Granted," said Gallant. Taking a great gulp of coffee, he added, "And get a pair of Hawkeyes up."

"Aye aye, sir."

A few minutes later, the OOD ordered, "Launch Hawkeyes."

Several hours later, the first Hawkeye reported, "Sixty auxiliary ships are orbiting Charlie."

Kelsey, who was in the second Hawkeye, reported, "One carrier, two battlecruisers, twelve cruisers, and thirty-two destroyers are in orbit six light-minutes from Charlie."

The OOD said, "That's the escort force protecting the Titan landing zones, sir. The carrier is the *Wwrath*." He struggled with the pronunciation of the Titan name.

Gallant thought, *It's a target-rich environment.*

Kelsey reported, "They don't appear to be at battle stations."

Thanks to its elliptical trajectory and the sun's corona, it looked like Task Force 34 had achieved surprise.

"I'm playing hide and seek with their sensors, but I can maintain stealth and continue to collect intelligence," said Kelsey.

Gallant winced at the risk she was taking but said nothing. If Kelsey could get targeting information, it would make his fighters, and bombers that much more effective.

He ordered, "Prepare Squadrons 6 and 8 for an all-out attack on the enemy carrier group. We'll deal with the auxiliary ships and the Titan landing forces once we've smashed the *Wwrath*."

Gallant spoke over the ship's intercom, "Men and women of the *Constellation*, I am honored to be leading you today. Our mission is to relieve the 2nd Marine Division on Charlie. The strong Titan ground forces are delivering punishing blows to our men and women. A carrier task force is protecting the sixty auxiliary ships supporting those troops. Our job is to destroy that carrier so we can land the 3rd Marine Division. We will not fail."

He listened to the buzz around the bridge. They were ready and determined.

Gallant thought, *I must trust that good leaders will get the job done.*

A few minutes later, he ordered, "Launch starfighters!"

Ryan felt the weight of acceleration as his Viper was shot out. He maneuvered into the wingman position behind his Squadron Leader, Edward Decatur.

Eight minutes later, thirty-six fighters were in position.

Lorelei sat in her Viper II. She hardly had a moment before the trigger was pulled and her ship whipped into space. The inky black surrounded her, sending a tingle along her spine.

After another eight minutes, thirty-six bombers were in formation, and the carrier-wing was on its way.

Everyone was raring to go on the sortie, but it took three hours for the starfighters to reach the *Wwrath* task force.

Circling nearby in her Hawkeye, Kelsey reported, "Squadron Leaders, I have critical targeting data. Standby for download."

Lorelei stared at the radar display and armed her weapon systems. She loaded the detailed targeting information and assigned her bombers. Her plasma cannon booted up along with the missile-select console. She ordered, "Flight leaders, follow the attack vectors for plan Alpha. Press your attack home."

The Titan sensors picked up the starfighters in time to launch their own fighters. The escorts put up a wall of flak and released decoys.

Decatur ordered, "Flight 1 punch a hole through the CSP. Flight 2 fly close bomber support. Flight 3 remain in reserve."

A moment later, Lorelei ordered, "Execute targeting plan Alpha."

The squadrons went into action and closed on the enemy. The pilots were determined to reach the *Wwrath*.

"Lock weapons on target," ordered Decatur, as his fighters surged forward engaging the enemy fighters.

"Fire!"

The tac1 chatter was getting started.

"Hey. I need help," screamed Flannery.

Ryan executed a hard turn to come to his aid. The power curve lit up and turned red; it was off the charts. He watched as the display showed the attack vector. It took a second before he reached the engagement envelope. He felt a momentary flash of admiration for the alien pilot. He was good. Finally, Ryan got a lock and fired. It was a hit.

"Poor bastard," said Ryan.

"Thanks," said Flannery.

The escort vessels' point defenses were able to throw up a lot of fire as the fighters closed.

"Look out, Hotshot, incoming," yelled Ryan.

Decatur's fighter took a direct hit and exploded.

During battle, there was no time for grief. As his wingman, Ryan became acting squadron leader.

A few minutes later, the fighters succeeded in punching a hole in the Titan fighter cover, and the cloud of enemy fighters split into smaller groups. Leaving the door open for the bombers.

Lorelei led one flight of bombers through the gap.

"Concentrate on the carrier."

"Incoming flak."

"Engage the point defense."

They faced decoys, jamming, and point defense, but they managed to launch twelve missiles toward the carrier.

"I got a hit," yelled one pilot.

One Titan destroyer put itself between the carrier and the missiles and was obliterated. Yet several missiles struct home and the *Wwrath* was wounded. She would never get a chance to launch bombers against the *Constellation*.

The starfighters returned home to rearm for another strike.

In all, Task Force 34 flew 259 sorties against the Titan carrier force. This weight of attack neutralized her as a threat. After a long day of fighting, the carrier was left a disabled wreck along with many of its escort vessels.

Task Force 34 moved closer to engage the enemy escort ships.

Gallant signaled, "All ships close on the enemy. *Indefatigable* and *Indomitable,* commence firing!"

The OOD reported, "Their destroyers are forming a defensive line. Enemy cruisers have launched a salvo of missiles."

Gallant ordered, "Launch decoys."

The decoys gave the Titans many more targets. They were forced to switch from passive to active sensors. Once the active sensors lit off, they became priority targets.

"Concentrate fire on missiles with active sensors."

The fighting was swift and violent as the fleets

passed each other. An enemy ship's shields buckled and collapsed.

The last two remaining enemy cruisers launched a salvo at the *Indefatigable.* She suffered minor damage. One Titan ship slipped through the defenses and hit the *Indefatigable* with an armor-piercing missile.

But the Titans were outmatched. The shields collapsed on the last disabled enemy battlecruiser. Blossoming clouds of debris erupted after each explosion. The ship shuddered and began breaking apart. Survival pods were launched.

The remaining Titan ships tried to break contact and escape. The *Indefatigable* and *Indomitable* tore through space and finished off the last of the enemy escort vessels.

Next, Task Force 34 moved into striking position and attacked the assault transports and supply ships around Charlie. They concentrated on the defenders around the satellite and engaged two enemy ships.

Gallant watched the battle play out. He trusted the task force to follow directions, but they also took advantage of opportunities without waiting for him.

The remaining Titan auxiliary ships were intercepted. And as the last ship was being destroyed, Gallant ordered a bombing raid on Charlie to relieve the pressure on the Marines. The battlecruiser's railguns struck the fixed targets with devasting effect.

Lorelei led the bombers on a run against ground targets. The flight had dropped their load and was swinging to return to the carrier when Lorelei was struck by a laser artillery battery. Her ship lost power and flew a ballistic trajectory down toward the planet.

Lorelei yelled, "Mayday! Mayday!"

CHAPTER 27

Crash

"**M**ayday. Mayday," shouted Lorelei over the transmitter. "My location is north forty-four degrees, twelve minutes, east 11 degrees, thirty-one minutes. Ship disabled and going down."

Her Viper II took several laser blasts that damaged the engine and blew a hole in the side of the ship. She struggled to maintain control over the dive, repeating her message several times. Plunging toward the surface, she kept up the routine but gritted her teeth when she got no response.

"Where are you, Lucky?" she muttered. "Thank goodness for my GPS beacon."

Lorelei used her considerable skills to bring the damaged Viper to a controlled crash on the rough surface of Charlie. She zipped up her flight suit and sealed her helmet. Then she forced the canopy open and painfully climbed out.

The wind kicked up a whirl of dust as she walked away, but her bruised body found each step painful.

A few minutes later, a thunderous explosion finished her ship.

Lorelei looked back at the crash site and watched lava ooze against the nearby rocks. A light breeze blew a concoction of molten titanium and lava ash in her direction.

She scanned the horizon, and through the hazy mist, she saw a bunker nestled against a cliff a klick away. She also saw far away shapes. Since she was in no man's land, they were most likely hostile.

Her instinct told her to run.

She ran.

It was a halting faulty kind of running, but at least she was moving.

Distant Titans soldiers shot at her, and she fired back until her handgun was completely discharged.

The area offered little cover, but if she could get to the bomb-damaged bunker, she would have a chance.

She counted her steps to distract her from the pain and plodded onward until miraculously she stumbled up to the bunker airlock. The automatic system was out, but she was able to manually open the outer hatch. Cycling through the compartment, she heard the click of the hatch closing followed by the hiss of fresh air.

Once inside, she tasted a strange mixture of air

elements. She found a place to rest. Reaching into a pocket, she pulled out an energy bar. She should have had a medi-kit as well, but she had failed to put one in her pocket in her haste to get on the mission. An omission she now regretted. She considered going back to the remains of the Viper to try and find the survival pack she had forgotten when she ran from the ship.

No, the open ground would mean death if she tried it. But maybe the Titans would find something better to do than chase her.

Lorelei let her mind wander as she tried to forget her problems. She let out another sigh at the memory of how comfortable and mundane her life had once been—when she was in school—when poetry was her most passionate interest. Still, it was a welcome distraction from the hardship she endured now, to recall the melodious lines she had once fashioned.

She sat in the center of the bunker looking around to see if there was anything useful lying about. She pulled down the top of her pressure suit and dressed her wounds as best she could.

A mouthful of water helped ease the sandpaper texture of her throat. She used the cold soapy water to rinse off her injuries. For a moment, she was mesmerized by the water swirling down the drain. As she dried off, she felt the damp, cold air around her. She started to relax when she heard an outside noise.

She called, "Whose there?"

There was no answer.

Pulling up her suit, she called once more, "Whose there?"

Still no response. She entered the next room.

She picked up her gun before she remembered it was empty. As her hand reached to open the hatch to the backroom, she heard a noise from the front entrance. The latch clicked.

"Who's there?" she called, in a raspy voice.

She took a few steps toward the front entrance then hesitated. The hatch didn't swing open.

Before she could decide what to do, she heard another click.

That's odd.

She walked quickly over to a monitor, but it wasn't working.

Jiggling the latch to the front hatch, she turned back toward the side door but stopped in her tracks when she heard a ratcheting sound coming from that direction.

Now she was fully alert.

Someone is out there!

Her self-control was wearing thin. She strode to the inside hatch and yanked it open. The airlock was empty. As she closed the hatch, out of the corner of her eye, she caught a glimpse of motion in a viewport blister.

She took a step and then heard the back-hatch cycle open and shut.

Lorelei gasped and bolted to the back room. She felt the pang of raw, cold fear—like a child's fear of a monster behind the closet door.

She clenched her knife and held it out in front of her. Her mouth was dry. She licked her lips, fighting down terror. One slow, cautious step after another, she crept toward the back airlock. She reached to open the inner hatch when someone grabbed her from behind.

"Aah!"

The hand holding her was powerful, but a familiar voice said, "I won't harm you. You're safe. It's me."

Twisting out of his grip, she stared in shock. Her surprise couldn't have been greater. Her emotional state changed from dread to joy.

"James!"

Steward's blue eyes twinkled. He said pleasantly, as if it was a perfectly ordinary circumstance, "I was in the neighborhood and thought I'd stop by."

She hadn't spoken to him in a year, and she hadn't dared imagine that she would ever see him alive.

"You gave me such a fright!" she said, her eyes wide and her hands clamped over her mouth.

"Sorry for sneaking around, but I had to make sure the coast was clear before I came in."

He gave a mocking bow. "Am I forgiven?"

She stammered, "Yes. Yes, of course."

They stood staring at each other for a long moment. The sight of his broad shoulders and warm smile flooded her mind with memories. She always felt safe with her big brother around.

"You haven't changed," she said, biting her

lower lip. "Couldn't you at least send word you were still alive every now and then?"

"It's not easy to send messages from here."

"How did you find me?"

"Your transponder showed a pilot was down in my backyard. I didn't know it was you until I saw you."

"I'm so glad you've come to rescue me."

"Oh. I can't say that you're rescued just yet."

"Why not?"

"We're in the middle of no man's land, and I've only a few men with me. They're outside keeping watch. We'll have a long way to go before you're safe."

"Shouldn't we get going then?"

He laughed. "You always were naive."

BOOM!

An explosion rattled the bunker.

Sonny burst in the bunker. "They're coming!"

CHAPTER 28

Counterstrike

Shuttlecraft filled with men and women remained attached to the transport vessels in orbit over Charlie. They were waiting breathlessly for the signal to land in hostile territory. An 80 km stretch along the northern and southern borders of a mountain range was chosen as respective landing zones, Whiskey and X-ray. A successful landing depended on the establishment of secure lodgments. From there, they could expand the beachhead and buildup supplies.

But the Titans were ready. They planted barbed wire and stake obstacles to make it dangerous for the shuttles to land. They were entrenched in bunkers filled with laser artillery and missiles. They had a stranglehold on the 2nd Marines, and they didn't intend to let go.

"How soon can you get here?" asked General

McIntyre over the erratic videoconference connection to the *Constellation*.

Gallant's rapid mind flew to reconsidering the cold math of the logistics. Forty transports prepared to send waves of troops into a heavily defended territory. Each shuttle carried a platoon and its gear. Every group of ten shuttles was accompanied by an auxiliary fire support platform. A guide shuttle ensured unit integrity and was available to collect escape pods when necessary. A Viper pair was assigned to each transport to provide escort and close fire support. Each landing zone was targeted by a cruiser-destroyer team for targeted bombardment. A long litany of prioritized targets was scheduled to be eliminated before landings started. Enemy flak, headquarters, and missile and laser batteries were on the top of that list. Local heavy weapons and tanks were also essential to allow the Marines a chance to grab a foothold. He considered every asset he could use as leverage to ensure a successful landing.

He said, "The bombardment will continue for three more hours. We're trying to take out as many hard weapon systems as possible before we send in soft bodies."

McIntyre chuckled. "I appreciate that, but my guys are holding on by the skin of their teeth. The fourth and eighth regiments have been overrun, and I preside over more no man's land than Marine held territory."

McIntyre recommended that the 3rd Marines

land some twenty klicks south of the original line. Once they consolidated a bridgehead, they could move against the forces surrounding the second division. The commander of the 3rd Marine Division interrupted, "My guys are ready to hit the landing zones as soon as the Commodore gives us the go-ahead."

"I've authorized paratroopers and special forces to begin operations inside of no man's land to relieve some of the pressure," said Gallant. "Bombardment targeting has been adjusted to give them a window for their mission."

"Thank you," said McIntyre, the strain in his voice was evident. "I know you kicked butt up there, Commodore, but down here the Titans are still full of fight and as mean as ever."

The following three hours might have seemed an eternity to the Marines on Charlie, but finally, Gallant said, "Go!"

The word rang in the ears of every shuttle pilot. Without hesitation, they flew to their objective. The ground fire was thick, but despite the mounting losses, the landings continued. First came a wave of engineer and demolition teams to remove obstacles and clear the area of mines. Next, Wave after wave of Marines hit the ground running. Tanks followed the initial assault battalions. The sooner they could construct rough roads, the faster the 3rd Marines could push outward from the landing zones.

Later that day, the 3rd Marine Division began to

penetrate the Titan position. Air support and shuttles moved troops and special forces throughout no man's land.

Sitting on the bridge, Gallant found himself going through the mental exercise. Circumstance favored the Titans. He wanted to consider actions he might take to shave some of those advantages down. He began playing 'What if' games. What if the Marines were unable to dislodge the Titan soldiers? What if Graves failed to arrive in time to stop Zzey? What if the Titan fleet received reinforcements? Of course, there was always one 'What if' too many.

To Gallant, the exercise of analysis cleared his mind and let him pursue lines of reasoning that he might not have otherwise considered.

He found himself wondering what Admiral Zzey might be thinking.

The *Warrior* was following Zzey in stealth mode and sending reports of his movements. Zzey's fleet of four carriers, six dreadnaughts, and escorts would reach Charlie in less than five days.

The third fleet consisted of three carriers, four dreadnaughts, and two battlecruisers. But despite its strength, the third fleet was not well-placed to deal with the threat of the Titan fleet. It was 1.5 light-days away from Charlie. It was up to Task Force 34 to delay the enemy long enough for the third fleet to catch up with events.

Gallant received a flash message from Admiral Graves telling him that the third fleet wouldn't face the Titan fleet. He ordered Task Force 34 to abandon the Marines and rejoin the third fleet.

Gallant remained in deep thought. He saw the fundamental defect of the situation. There was no single command due to the distances separating the forces and the time delay in translating any orders into action. He couldn't unite with the third fleet, if it meant leaving the auxiliary ships to their fate.

After racking his brain for a solution, Gallant came to a fateful decision. With the landings well underway, he left a small cruiser-destroyer detachment at Charlie to cover the landings. He intended to lead Task Force 34 toward Zzey's fleet of carriers.

The thought came to him that he might have only a few minutes remaining as the captain of the *Constellation*. He decided to embark on a course of action that could prove ill-conceived. It would take a great many tenuous things to come together for his plan to succeed.

He approached the ship's executive officer on the bridge. He chose to have this conversation in the open, rather than in the privacy of his cabin, for good tactical reasons. "Commander Fletcher, will you read these orders? I am having difficulty interpreting how to carry them out. I would appreciate your council."

He handed the tablet to the XO and waited while she read, reread, and then read the orders yet again.

"It is a clear-cut order from Admiral Graves ordering Task Force 34 to leave Charlie, circumvent the Titans, and rejoin the third fleet."

If he had a grain of sense, he would stop the conversation there. He would take some time to find another path forward. He could simply walk away from the XO.

He asked, "Do you understand the ramification for the Marines if I carry out those orders?"

Sensing the tension on the bridge, several of the crew turned toward them.

Fletcher frowned. "If you refuse to obey a direct order from Admiral Graves, it would be my duty to relieve you of command."

He knew Fletcher couldn't remove him from command without a direct order from Graves and that would take considerable time. Yet, he was conscious of a trembling in his neck. It was not fear, for he trusted in his decision to broach this subject. It was tension creeping up his spine. He had to play his hand accurately, or he could face misfortune.

"Commander, you wanted command of this carrier from the very beginning," said Gallant. The tenor of his voice was quiet and respectful. "And though you and I have very different leadership styles, I believe you are as dedicated to this crew and its mission, as I am."

She looked skeptical, examining the nuance in his words.

Then as if seeing her for the first time, he touched her arm and said, "You would be an outstanding captain."

Fletcher visibly straightened and pulled her shoulders back.

He said, "It would take a captain and crew of unbridled courage to defend Charlie in the face of Zzey's fleet."

The Officer of the Deck took a step closer to the captain and the executive officer.

Gallant asked in a loud, forceful voice, "If you were in command right now, would you abandon the Marines?"

The tension on the bridge was now unpalatable.

Gallant leaned closer to her and whispered, "Would you, Margret?"

Margret Fletcher fell into a swirl of confusing conflicting emotions. The struggle between ambition and duty played out on her face. She looked at her captain and blinked once.

They stood in a standoff for several minutes. Her eyes searched the anxious faces surrounding her on the bridge.

Licking her lips, she said, "You know, Henry, I never concluded my investigation into Titan sabotage of our communication systems. This flash message might be a ruse. The Titan's may have found a way to sabotage our communications and mislead us. We should send a message back to Admiral Graves asking to have this message authenticated. Of course, even at the speed of light that would take 24 hours for the round trip."

Gallant knew in a flash that he had won her

over. He would never doubt her again.

He said, "Thank you for your council."

But that didn't change his options, to fight or let Charlie face a terrible outcome. Badly outnumbered, he knew any victory here would be purchased at great cost.

The enemy was closing at a steady pace, confident that Task Force 34 was trapped, and the outcome was inevitable.

Gallant would have to find a way to fool the enemy into making a misstep.

A forlorn hope?

"I beg your pardon, sir," said Midshipman Logan as Gallant entered CIC.

"Yes, Mr. Logan?"

"Are you okay, sir. You aren't looking well."

"Is that your professional diagnosis?"

"It's just that you've been up every minute that I have for the last few days and I don't think you went to sleep when I did. You're doing too much, sir."

"That's a strange thing for an officer to suggest, Mr. Logan. But I can assure you I am fit to perform my duties."

"Of course, sir. I didn't mean to imply otherwise. But you should get some rest."

"Thank you. I'll turn in as soon as you fill me in on your progress with the drones."

Logan said, "I've been working with the CIC

data techs, and we've unpacked the data that the *Warrior* found. So far, we've identified the Chameleons ship info."

Gallant looked at the young man and said, "Go on."

"Captain, I found a deep space signal in one of the recordings, and I've been working on decrypting the signal using our AI computer."

Gallant was impressed with Logan's initiative.

"What does a deep space signal have to do with the local battle?" asked Gallant

"Everything."

"You'll have to explain that."

Logan licked his lips and took a deep breath to gather his wits. "I've decrypted a pattern in communications and decoded their point of origin. I know where the Chameleon home star system is."

"That's great. Why didn't you say that?" asked Gallant. "We can use the alien characteristics in drones to fool Titans. And we can transmit signals from the direction of the Chameleon home star to add to the credibility."

"I'll get to work on that, sir."

CHAPTER 29

Search and Rescue

R yan asked, "I request permission to lead a SAR for our downed pilot on Charlie, sir?"

Gallant sat in his cabin with his dark eyes lowered. Absurdly, he was jealous. The desire for combat was steadfast in his psyche. Leading an elite squad far behind enemy lines was the kind of assignment he thrived on. It was representative of the madness of war that Ryan would seek out a dangerous mission while Gallant bitterly resented being left behind. That was, of course, philosophically absurd.

"What do you propose?" asked Gallant eager to wade into the details of the adventure.

"Lorelei Steward's transponder gives her location as a bunker in no man's land. It could be several days before the third Marines can get there. I could take a Marine paratroop platoon and recover her in a few hours, sir."

Gallant considered refusing the request. He

couldn't afford to leave his best pilot behind when he was going to be fighting Zzey very soon. Then it occurred to him, what would he do if it were Alaina who was lost in enemy territory. Would any order keep him from trying to rescue her?

"You've earned that right," said Gallant. "Get your team together and conduct a search and rescue for Ensign Steward. I want you both back safe and sound. I'm going to need you very soon."

He put the thought of losing them out of his mind.

The desert plain of Charlie was the color of heat, khaki topaz. The surrounding volcanoes spewed hot molten rock into the atmosphere like heating vents pouring fiery plumes. The wispy atmosphere carried streaming currents of toxic gases. It was an environment that required all Ryan's skill to navigate.

He flew a Cobra-787 jet with a one-hundred-meter cable trailing behind it. Tethered to the cable was one squad of para-marines. When the Cobra reached Lorelei's GPS coordinates, he identified a firefight. The Marines in the bunker were surrounded by Titans in the hills.

He flew the Cobra at two kilometers over the ground several hundred meters from the bunker.

"Sergeant, ready?" he asked.

"Ready."

"Go," he ordered.

The para-marine squad released their tether hooks and fell. They ignited their jet packs and flew to the ground, landing together in a coordinated formation. Once on the ground, they spread out into a defensive perimeter.

Titan soldiers closed in on the position.

The Marines showed their famous grit by fighting against the strength of the Titan ground forces.

Ryan flew overhead and fired his Cobra's twin Gatling guns at Titan targets. The Gatling spewed 1,000 rounds per minute at the enemy, ripping apart everything in their path.

-rat-tat-tat! -rat-tat-tat! -rat-tat-tat! -rat-tat-tat!

A one-hundred-meter tower bristling with machine guns and heavy weapons rose into the middle of the area. Ryan used it for target practice, letting the Gatling guns slice it apart, target eliminated.

-rat-tat-tat! -rat-tat-tat! -rat-tat-tat! -rat-tat-tat!

The Cobra made pass after pass ripping the Titan position and destroying an artillery emplacement. Soon the Titans in the immediate area retreated.

The para-marines secured a section of flat terrain and cleared an area for the Cobra to land. Ryan landed several hundred meters from the bunker.

"Do you see anything?" he asked.

"Looks clear," said the sergeant.

Ryan hesitated a moment, but decisions had to be made.

"Come on!" he said, charging toward the bunker.

CHAPTER 30

Foxy

This close to the sun, the solar flare had the same effect as a hurricane on the *Constellation's* sensors. The micro-meteors struck inconsequentially against the Titanium hull, but they were a nuisance interfering with receiving accurate information from the long-range sensor probes. Drones and Hawkeyes stretched the ship's vision, but Gallant wasn't satisfied. He walked the deck of the bridge reexamining his decision to change course. He could feel the ship's vibrations shift, ever so slightly, as the ship maneuvered. The task force was twelve light-hours away from Charlie and only six light-hour away from Zzey's fleet. They had been on a collision course until this last turn when the task force made a ninety-degree turn away from the sun. Gallant had deliberately turned off stealth mode on all ships. Zzey had no trouble seeing the visible light from his ships. The question was, would Zzey turn to intercept or continue straight to Charlie.

The watch-standers were quiet and reflective, sensitive to their captain's mood. His hands locked behind his back; Gallant increased his pace though he could only walk five steps toward the bulkhead before he had to turnaround again. It seemed a futile activity, yet he couldn't calm himself enough to sit still in the command chair.

He waited. Zzey wouldn't even know that Task Force 34 had turned for another six hours, and Gallant wouldn't know Zzey's response for six hours after that. Even a message from the *Warrior* wouldn't arrive any earlier.

Why is light so slow!

He spent the next eight hours on the bridge directing normal ship activities. Then finally, he left the bridge and went to his cabin and threw himself on the cot determined to get some rest. He lay listening to all the scratching, tapping, and flowing sounds of the ship, dismissing each in turn. But his restless mind refused to shut itself off.

He marshaled his thoughts. What were the Titans' plans? Were they ready for an all-out engagement? What new resource could he create? For some time, his mind wrestled with finding a solution until he finally drifted off into a fitful sleep.

An alert bell sounded over his cot.

Startled, he jumped up; his half-closed eyes searched the dark. "Yes? What?"

Over the intercom, the OOD said, "The Titan fleet turned, sir. Our farthest Hawkeye got a brief glimpse which was confirmed minutes later by a message from the *Warrior*. They're still trailing Zzey."

"Damn and blast it, man! Don't you know how to give a proper report? Which way did they turn?"

Gallant instantly regretted his words. There was nothing gained by bulling the officer.

"My apologies, sir," said the OOD. "The Titan fleet was 4.8 light-hours from Task Force 34 at the time of the turn. They are paralleling our course heading away from the sun at 0.2 C."

Gallant was relieved that the enemy had taken the bait. Now it was a game of hide-and-seek.

"Are there any Titan drones or recon ships in the area?" he asked.

"There is a drone heading toward us, but it is beyond our CSP range."

"Very well. Keep me informed."

Gallant lay down for several minutes, wondering if there was any chance, he could return to sleep. There was not. He was on the bridge ten minutes later.

"What do you think, Commander?"

Fletcher looked worn and rumpled, but Gallant wasn't about to comment on that.

She said, "I expect we can keep Zzey entertained for a while, but I don't think he will let the third fleet get significantly closer before he brings things to a climax."

"I agree. Even so, we'll play this out." He knew there would be a clash before too long, but any delay would be beneficial to his long-term plan.

She nodded and returned to staring at the AI readout.

A few minutes later, another Hawkeye got a glimpse and reported that Zzey was steady on a parallel course, one point off the starboard beam.

Pointing to the status board, Fletcher said, "There he is."

That gesture epitomized navy life—a moment of decision, followed by excitement, hustle, and an enemy's reaction. Then the two fleets would thrash along and settle down waiting until the next decision had to be made.

"Sir? Are we leaving the Marines?" asked the OOD. All hands on the bridge were listening.

"We're moving away from Charlie only so long as the Titans follow us. We will always remain between them and the Marines. Any man who thinks there is another way to perform his duty should speak up now?"

Every head on the bridge shook enthusiastically.

Gallant said, "Officer of the Deck, pass the word that off-duty personnel are to rest. This chase—this game—will continue for many hours before we'll see action."

"Aye, aye sir."

Gallant remained on the bridge for several hours before he went for a tour of the ship's spaces to see how the crew was reacting.

"Are you worried?" he asked a young seaman.

"Not me, sir. I know you'll get us through."

Many in the crew repeated this. While the crew's confidence was comforting, he wondered if he would be able to live up to their expectations.

The next location report from the *Warrior* was troubling. Zzey was no longer satisfied paralleling the task force's course. He increased speed to 0.25C and turned several degrees toward the task force. At the rate of closure, they would be within engagement range before another day. The Titan's four carriers and six dreadnaughts would make short work of the *Constellation* and her few escorts.

Gallant said, "Officer of the Deck, all ahead full, accelerate to 0.25 C. Steady on course ten degrees to port."

That would put them on a parallel course with Zzey once more.

Zzey had managed to close the distance, but Gallant had a few tricks left.

Several hours later, Zzey changed course, hard to port, closing the track.

Fletcher said, "He could be daring us."

"Yes. He's clever. He wants us to reveal our hand. If we maintain course, we'll increase our distance from him, but we'll give him an opening to cut us off from Charlie. If I immediately turn toward Charlie, he'll know that I consider a threat to Charlie as paramount. At that point, he'll stop chasing us and head directly for Charlie knowing we'll be forced to commit to battle on his terms."

"We have no choice. We have to throw ourselves in front of Charlie," said Fletcher, her voice breaking.

"Eventually, we'll do that. But do the math. We have enough of an angle advantage on Zzey such that we can reach Charlie before him. In fact, let's give Zzey something to think about."

"Officer of the Deck, starboard twenty degrees. Come to an intercept course with the third fleet."

Fletcher said, "I don't understand. Just yesterday, you refused to circumvent the Titans and join the third fleet. You practically pleaded with me to avoid that."

"Admiral Zzey doesn't know that. If it looks like I am abandoning the Marines to unite with the third fleet, what do you think Zzey will do?"

"He has the option of smashing the Marines, but that would allow our forces to face him as a unified fleet."

"Yes. He might be satisfied to smash the Marines and leave the system without engaging our full force. I can't risk him doing that, but so long as we have a better closing angle to Charlie than Zzey, I can tempt him into revealing his priority."

A couple of hours later, Zzey changed course, but it was a puzzling change because it neither closed on Charlie nor tried to intercept Task Force 34.

Gallant chuckled. He ordered the *Constellation* to head toward Charlie.

Fletcher looked puzzled.

"He's foxy. All our sensors are reporting that his fleet is moving in our general direction, but not at an optimal intercept course."

"What does that mean?"

"It means he doesn't want to intercept any time soon. At the same time, he's minimizing his travel to Charlie. I'll bet you a month's pay that he's detached his dreadnaughts to attack Charlie along with our auxiliaries and escorts. They can smash the Marines. All the while, his carriers will keep their option open to fight us or the third fleet."

"Of course! You're right. So now, we'll have to rush to Charlie and fight part, or all, of Zzey's fleet."

"I'm afraid so. The *Warrior* will probably send us a detailed update before long. But this game of ours has bought us some time. I'm hoping it was enough."

"Enough for what?" asked Fletcher.

CHAPTER 31

Getting Out Alive

R yan and the para-marines crawled across the
rough terrain until they reached a ridge. They
spread out around its base as enemy ground
forces infiltrated the area. Soon the two groups were
engaged in close combat.

"Covering fire," shouted the sergeant.

Gunfire erupted from the Marines and the sergeant sprinted ahead a dozen meters and then hit the
deck.

"Next group," he shouted. "Covering Fire!"

The next team sprang up and ran to the sergeant.

The next time the sergeant yelled, Ryan jumped
up and ran.

Pfft! pfft! pfft!

The first bullet hit Ryan. It felt as if he was
kicked in the chest. He couldn't catch his breath.
Everything was spinning, and there was a roar in his

ears. He dropped to the ground clutching his chest, listening to the frantic thumping of his heart. He tried to keep his eyes open, but the area was a blur.

I need help.

A Marine hurried to his position and examined his chest. "You'll be fine. Your Kevlar vest stopped the bullet."

"Then why does my chest feel like it's got a hole in it?" asked Ryan.

"Here, I'll put a pain patch over it. You'll feel fine in a minute."

The Marine ministered to him and then went to attend another injured man.

Ryan's instinct was to go to Lorelei. But he couldn't move. He tried to get up but quickly fell back down. It took several minutes before he could catch his breath. Soon he was able to stand up and move again. He dashed toward the bunker with the Marines in fits and starts.

When they finally reached their destination, they were greeted by Captain James Steward at the bunker hatch.

"Man, am I glad to see you," said Steward.

Ryan asked, "Is Ensign Lorelei Steward here?"

"Here," said Lorelei, exiting the bunker.

Ryan grabbed her and hugged her.

Steward said, "You'd better unhand my sister, buddy."

The couple turned to Steward.

"This is the guy I was telling you about, James."

"So, I guessed," laughed Steward. "What's the

plan? The Titans have us pinned down from the surrounding hills. Their firepower is intense and growing."

"I don't have much of a plan for getting out. I mostly concentrated on getting here," said Ryan.

"If we wait here, they'll build up strength, and we'll be in worse shape."

"I guess we're between a rock and a hard place," said the sergeant.

Steward nodded, "Then maybe we need to find some wiggle room between that rock and a hard place."

Ryan said, "If we can get everyone to my Cobra, they could hook up to the tether, and I'll fly us out."

"We need to be quick before the Titans rally and return with reinforcements," said the sergeant.

They leapfrogged out of the area and back to the Cobra.

Pling! pling! pling!

Every dozen meters was a challenge.

Pfft! pfft! pfft!

But soon the team and the survivors were aloft attached to the end of a long cable flying below Ryan's Cobra.

CHAPTER 32

Chameleon

For some time, Gallant lay stretched out on his cot in the semi-dark. He would have preferred to sleep, but his active mind wouldn't relax. He considered getting up and going onto the bridge, but he would only spread his tension to the crew. So, he lay flat on his back with his hands behind his head in a futile effort to unwind. The sounds he heard told him the ship was operating normally. One meter from his cot was a stand with a monitor that could show every vital parameter on the 160,000-ton vessel. If that wasn't reassuring enough, ten meters from his cabin door was an OOD who would alert him at the slightest hint of a problem. Most captains would have considered that ample insurance to permit a restful sleep. But the prolonged engagement with the Zzey fleet was providing some of the worst stress Gallant had ever experienced. So, he remained restless and lost in thought.

Zzey is coming.

Gallant was sure of that. Zzey would not retreat. After all, the Titan had invested a great many resources to secure this system. But he wished that Admiral Graves would act more aggressively. He was left with the consequences of his unfulfilled wish. He should have foreseen that the *Constellation* would be left on her own.

Fortunately, he had a team of able professionals around him. As the commander of a task force at the forefront of the battle, it was his responsibility to see that they acquitted themselves well. He reassured himself that they would do so.

What he couldn't understand was why his judgment had been so faulty in another matter of consequence. He had allowed his duty to safeguard the Marines, blind him to the possibility that Graves might not be as committed.

There was a knock on his cabin door.

"Enter."

Logan took two steps into the cabin and said, "Midshipman Logan, reporting as ordered, sir,"

"At ease," said Gallant, leaning back in his wooden chair. "What is the status of your project?"

"Sir, I've completed the data analysis and software coding. The AI is in the process of completing the simulations module."

"Have you run a drone test?"

"Yes, sir." Logan grinned, proud of himself. "The test was successful. Our sensors tracked the 'Chameleon carrier' at a range of two light-hours and couldn't identify it as a drone."

"What about dreadnaughts and cruisers simulations?"

"Ah ... I haven't tested those yet, sir."

"How long before a full set of drones will be ready to deploy?"

Logan looked baffled as if this was the first, he had heard of the request.

Gallant said, impatiently, "These aren't toys, Mr. Logan. Didn't you think we would need them?"

"Well, sir. I didn't expect it would be so soon."

Gallant cast a stern look and asked, "Midshipman Logan, how much more time do you need to deploy the decoy drones?"

Logan stood still, looking like he had lost his way in a complicated math problem. "Manufacture of the chips and the final installation into all the available drones could take several days. But thirty drones could be ready tomorrow if you give me several more computer techs and half-a-dozen engineering techs."

"I will give you all the support you need, but I want fifty operational drones available by 1200 hours tomorrow."

Logan worked his jaw, but words didn't come out.

"Well, Mr. Logan?"

"Aye, aye, sir."

"He's turned, Captain,"

Gallant examined the three-dimensional star plot. Fletcher pointed at the red line as it shifted position. Everyone on the bridge craned their necks to get a glimpse.

The Titan admiral knew his business. Zzey had sacrificed distance for the angle of approach. Mathematically, he was in the perfect position to turn directly for Charlie and force Gallant's hand.

Here was the moment of danger. If the *Constellation* failed to gain the inside position, Zzey would deliver a catastrophic blow to the Marines on Charlie before they could intervene.

If the *Constellation* did gain the inside position, Zzey could deliver his violent blow on her instead. Gallant had a good ship and well-trained crew, but the sheer numbers would likely prevail. Odds of four-to-one in carriers were greater than advisable to risk. He might have the distinction of becoming a modern-day 'Horatius at the Bridge.' A distinction he would avoid, if possible.

His plan had to be carried out to perfection to avoid a bad outcome.

He shook his head to clear away the black mood and said, "We've no choice. Helmsman; port twenty degrees, come to course two three zero."

"Port twenty degrees, coming to course two three zero, aye sir."

A minute later, the helmsman reported, "Steady on course two three zero, sir."

"Very well," said Gallant.

He turned to Midshipman Logan. "Is everything ready?"

The young man bit his lip and fidgeted. "All preparations are complete, Captain. They're ready to fly."

Gallant smiled as he noticed Logan's crossed fingers.

He ordered, "Flight Operations Officer, deploy all drones."

The main viewscreen showed each drone as it spewed out of the launch bay and headed on its secret journey.

A few minutes later, Logan reported, "Fifty drones have been launched and are in task force formation. They are using maximum stealth and will accelerate to 0.3 C over the next two hours."

"When will they reach the primary location?" asked Gallant.

Logan said, "They will be ready to drop cloak and transmit simulation signals at 2400 hours."

Fletcher asked, "How do you think the Titans will react?"

Gallant tore his mind away from the worrisome prospect that his charade would fail. He said, "We did what we had to do. Now we'll let the world adjust. Now comes the hard part, waiting to see if it works."

The Zzey fleet was only four light-hours from Charlie while the third fleet was still far away.

"It's 2400, sir."

The drone task force dropped its cloak and began transmitting. They appeared on sensor screens as a Chameleon fleet, ghost-like in the distance. They broadcast periodically in the direction of the Chameleon home star.

Gallant wondered what it was like on the bridge of the Titan flagship, *Vampiri*, when Admiral Zzey suddenly saw a large fleet of Chameleon ships heading toward him.

XO said, "That's got their attention. We've got them scared."

"Don't be so sure," said Gallant. "They're not panicking."

She asked, "What do we do next?"

"Accepting battle at the appropriate time and place is our best option to defeat the Titans. It all comes down to a timing thing. Giving relativistic effects, making changes too early will give the enemy time to react, too late, and the ships will never reach the proper position."

For over an hour, the Titans appeared uncertain how to respond. Then as the minutes passed, they accelerated to an intercept course toward the 'Chameleon fleet.'

At .2 C light-speed, it would take several hours to reach them.

"Sir, the *Warrior* reports that Zzey has launched fighters and bombers toward the 'Chameleon fleet.'"

Gallant analyzed the display screens. "That's what I was waiting for. They're at their most vulnerable. It's our best chance. We must fight while they have the fewest fighters to defend themselves. If we can't win, then we must make them suffer. Launch all fighters and bombers for an all-out strike against Zzey's carriers."

Ryan guided his Viper into the landing bay then sagged into his seat, refusing to move for several minutes. He was drained. He wanted to close his eyes and sleep in the cockpit, even though he had to get ready for a sortie in mere minutes. Somehow, he managed to open the hatch and get to the deck. His crew chief met him with a long list of questions about his Viper's performance and damage assessment.

Other ships were following him in and going through the process. He dragged himself to his stateroom and stripped. He got in the shower and let the hot water work its magic. Finally, he grabbed a stim bar and coffee and started to recover.

He couldn't believe it when moments later, his squadron was summoned to the flight deck. He swore. He had to go out again. His finger fumbled with his flight suit and went out. His chief was talking a mile a minute explaining what was fixed on the Viper and what was still in bad shape and had to be babied.

He fixed his gaze on Lorelei who emerged from the compartment hatch. She was limping surrounded by members of Squadron 8 patting her back to welcome her home.

After their escape from the warzone on Charlie, Ryan and Lorelei had flown a couple of Marine fighters at max thrust to reach the *Constellation*.

He said, "Lorelei, are you okay? Our squadrons must meet at rally point omega in twenty minutes."

She nodded, "Don't worry about me, Lucky."

He smiled.

That's what I like about her.

He took a moment to reflect on the last words Captain Gallant had said to him, "I'm assigning you as Squadron Leader 6. I trust that you will get your ships to target and back."

That's exactly what he intended to do.

Somewhere ahead lay the Titan fleet, but before they faced them, the lighthearted pilot checked his ships. He counted on luck as much as a skill to see him safely returning. When it was his turn, he gave the flight chief a thumb's up and felt the weight of 10 g's crush his chest.

At the rally point, the combat wing of the *Constellation* gathered into one large formation, the fighters in the lead.

The race was on. Zzey's combat wing was heading toward the 'Chameleon fleet,' and the *Constellation's* space wing was heading toward Zzey's fleet. It was a race that depended upon finely balanced timing. If surprise failed, Ryan would be out of position and outgunned.

Several hours later, they approached the enemy fleet.

"Lucky, we're closing fast," said Bear on tac 1.

"I can see that for myself," snapped Ryan. His tone exposed his raw nerves, but he ordered a change in formation into a fighting pyramid with the tip pointing at the enemy. The bombers were tucked away inside the configuration. If his surprise tactics worked, his reformed concentration would deliver a mighty blow.

"Look at that. Their CSP is totally confused. You've completely fooled them. The Titans must be boiling mad. They were waiting for our fighters to break off and engage in a dogfight. Now they'll have to attack directly into our overlaying defensive fire," said Bear.

The greatest gain possible was to keep the formation tight all the way toward the carriers. But Ryan knew that he would have to split the formation into separate attack flights to go after each of the carriers. That was the point of greatest vulnerability.

"Keep station. Prepare for Formation Zed four in thirty seconds," said Ryan.

A minute later, he yelled, "Execute."

Squadron 8 broke out of the cover provided by the fighters. The fighters engaged the Titan CSP.

"Weapons lock on target," said Bear. "Ready to fire."

Ryan smiled. "Fire."

"Direct hit."

Ryan recalled his combat experiences and felt the exhilarating rush of adrenalin as he anticipated the life-or-death gamble he faced.

As they fought off the first wave of attackers, a second group of Titan fighters was detected and intercepted.

Lucky ordered, "Send the bombers through the

gaps."

The bombers made their attack runs.

Lorelei led Squadron 8 into the clear.

She ordered, "Squadron 8, prepare to break into formation Delta."

A moment later, she said, "Execute."

The starfighters split into four flights and attacked. The Titans threw up a wall of flak.

Lorelei led flight one and though she concentrated on precision flying, dodging incoming missiles and Titan fighters caused her to miss her timing window. Unfortunately, she was forced to shift her position. She let her second take the lead, and she made a loop to fall in behind the last ship in the flight. After the entire flight launched their missiles, she began her run. The flak was heavier then. She had to dodge more anti-missiles and identify decoys and jammers.

She got a lock on the carrier and made sure she reached the release point. As soon as her missiles launched, she felt a release of tension because even if she were hit now, she had completed her mission.

Another flight of bombers followed. They released missiles that damaged several enemy carriers leaving them bleeding plasma.

The Viper IIs made hits on the flagship, *Vampiri*, and badly damaged a battlecruiser.

Lorelei reported, "Our scans show three Titan carriers hit. We've also identified several missile hits on two dreadnaughts."

They knew they had to get the mission done first. Everything else comes second. That includes getting back alive. They relaxed when the damage assessment showed a success and there was no hot pursuit. They got away clean. It was a clinical strike.

An hour later, the OOD reported, "The enemy fleet has changed course, sir."

Gallant rubbed his brow, studying the display screen. The enemy had been passive for some time, so this was unexpected.

"It's difficult to identify their destination. I suspect the last course change was intended to fight us. They still have a formable force of dreadnaughts and escorts. They're several light-hours away."

At .2 C it would take them several hours to reach us."

He pondered if he should wait for more information or act quickly.

If we approach each other at .2 C, a high-speed engagement would produce few significant hits. The relativistic distortion would be hard to counter. He needed to convince them to slow to engagement speed to fight properly.

The enemy ships started to brake and slowed significantly over the next hour. The minutes crawled by trying his patience.

"Adjust course to intercept. Prepare to engage."

"They've discovered our ruse with the drones too late. Most of their fighters were chasing ghosts while our carrier wing hit them where it hurt. We didn't destroy them, but we severely damaged three carriers. They're not going to be thinking of going on the offense anytime soon."

"They may be trying to delay contact for as long as possible."

Zzey abruptly broke off the fight.

Fletcher asked, "Aren't we going to chase Zzey and hit him again?"

"No," said Gallant.

That was the most sensible decision. Despite the successful bomber attack, they had only damaged three carriers. The remaining carrier was enough to even the odds against the *Constellation*. If the three carriers had been destroyed outright, he would have tried it. The fleets were close enough for continued action, but Zzey would have time to make some repairs. If the damaged carriers were able to recover, or if Zzey's six dreadnaughts could get into the action, Task Force 34 would be in trouble.

Gallant ordered, "Helmsman set course for Charlie."

Admiral Zzey's fleet left the Ross star system.

Drained by the emotional distress of battle, Gallant remained in his cabin all the next day. His muscles ached, his stomach clenched, and his eyes blurred. Emotional turmoil swamped him as he thought of those who he wouldn't see again. Their pleas for help replayed in his head. The bad moment lingered, and a shadow of sadness fell over him.

After a while, he returned his mind to his responsibilities.

He wrote the report number and date at the top of the page. He wrote "Sir" before he realized he could find the words to start his after-action report. He was sure that there would be many eyes from the admiralty reading what was written and that those words might find their way into the press, especially with the election so close. He told himself that he would write a simple, straightforward description of the situation, his actions, and leave it to others to decide if the outcome warranted condemnation or praise. But that was not an easy line to walk. He could imagine that there were those who no matter what he wrote would find flaws in his decisions and performance. After all, there could always be a better result in hindsight. He understood that a careless word from him could expose those he cared about to criticism, including Roberts, Collingsworth, and even the president.

Even more importantly, it would be read by the wives and family of the crews who fought, including Alaina. He didn't like the thought that they would be distressed by the reality of warfare, especially those who lost loved ones. But no matter the heartache, or the loss, he wouldn't stand down.

He was choked up for a while, and then the grief

abated. Soon ideas blended into words, and he wrote his battle report.

A week later, Admiral Graves and the Third Fleet arrived at Charlie.

CHAPTER 33

Home

When Gallant returned to Earth, he was sickened by the newscasts showing the tremendous loss of life in the Ross system. The families of fallen Marines and Sailors mourned their loved ones. Just as disappointing was the news touting the upcoming presidential election. Neumann was ahead in the polls, thanks in large part to Admiral Graves, the Hero of Ross, campaigning for him.

Graves' account of the battle at Ross was absurd in every detail; depicting Graves' brilliance in outmaneuvering and outfighting Titan Admiral Zzey. Just as ludicrous was his accusation leveled at Gallant for failing to obey orders in the face of the enemy.

Which was the greater lie?

Gallant sighed as he began packing his uniforms into a duffle bag in his cabin aboard the *Constellation*. He put in the essentials; clothes, hygiene prod-

H. Peter Alesso

ucts, and personal items. He touched the wedding and academy rings on his finger.

He looked around the small cabin where he spent so much time with uncertainty and worry. He wanted to remember this moment, to keep the idea of his command alive in his mind.

He told himself, he wanted to be treated fairly, but regardless, he would never doubt that he had acted as he thought best for his crew and his people. He was willing to face the consequences of his actions.

Glancing around the small room once more, he sighed, thinking back to how proud he had been when he moved in, even happier when he thought he was succeeding in his job. He recalled the many knocks on his door and his relationship with his crew. The memories made him feel lonely as dawned on him that this had been his home, and the crew had been his family for many stressful months. He was leaving something beautiful, something worthwhile. It all seemed in vain now, as if he had become tainted—ruined.

As he turned to go, he heard footsteps.

Fletcher walked to the open door and glanced at his bag.

"Captain? What are you doing? You're leaving?"

"No choice. You've received your orders to assume acting command of the Constellation?"

"Yes, but there is no need for you to leave until the court-martial is convened."

"I think we would both be better served if I was off the *Constellation*."

"Where will you go?"

He felt alone and devastated. "Do you mean, will I be arrested, and detained until trial?"

She nodded.

He wanted to ask her to take care of his people, but instead, he said, "I don't know. I'm going home to my wife. They can't take that away from me."

Gallant left the *Constellation*. His coveted command snatched away; he wondered what further punishment lay in store for him.

But no sooner had he landed at Melbourne then the military police arrested him. The arrest warrant charged him with crimes including failure to obey a lawful order of a superior in the face of the enemy (just one notch below treason), dereliction of duty, and a litany of lesser but just as malicious accusations that would total up to life in prison if convicted.

The officers placed him in handcuffs and led him to a police vehicle.

He found that prison hasn't changed in centuries. It remained a confined space with unyielding walls, callous guards, and harsh realities. The prison complex focused on ultimate control. Gallant was moved from place to place in handcuffs and leg shackles. Instead of long strides, he could only shuffle forward. Instead of swinging his arms, he held them awkwardly in front of him.

The prison was built with smoothly polished metal walls. It was a complex of interlocking structures where the prisoners were held in electronically controlled cells with force shields with video monitors. The guards were armed with stun guns and sonic whistles that could stun a person. Prison life sapped the will and deadened the spirit. There was no sympathy, empathy, or compassion inside its boundaries.

Gallant had to find his own way to retain his self-respect. For the most part, he remained compliant and obedient. Some prisoners he saw, cringed and showed empty lethargic eyes.

After two weeks of confinement, he was finally permitted a visit from his wife.

Alaina waited patiently behind a glass partition. She sat in front of him and spoke through a grill opening.

"Henry, are you okay?"

"I'm fine. How are you holding up?"

"I'm fine Dear, but I'm worried. The prosecutor got the judge to require a fortune for bail. I've taken out all our savings, and I hocked nearly everything that we have, and it still isn't enough. I tried to get a loan from the bank, but they practically laughed in my face. It turns out that 'no collateral and an accused felon' produces poor prospects for money lenders."

Her dry sarcasm made Gallant laugh.

"What about our jet-flyer?" he asked.

Alaina winced. She loved to fly that tiny craft. It was their only keepsake from Elysium.

She said, "That might be enough. I will sell it today."

A few days later, as Gallant exited the prison, he saw a look that spread across Alaina's face that was indescribable—it was as if she had just discovered 'love at first sight.'

He wrapped his arms around her. "Let's go home."

"My home is with you." Alaina put her arm around him.

The weather had transformed over the last weeks; the warm summer breeze had given way to a brisk rain. Likewise, Gallant felt transformed as he bound down the street a free man once more.

He marveled at every sight around him as if it were the first time he saw the town.

Over the next few days, he discovered that the Navy was withholding his pay pending the resolution of the trial. This forced Alaina to drop out of school to find a job since as an accused felon, he was unemployable.

It was a stormy day in Melbourne as the wind blew a light drizzle over Gallant and sending a chill up his spine. He crammed his hands deeper into his pockets and leaned against the wind. His eyes blinking, and his cheeks letting the water fall off his face.

It was a month since he was released from prison and he was walking along the road to the veteran's center.

"Henry. Henry, wait up. It's me."

Gallant turned. Facing into the wind, he saw John Roberts running toward him.

"It's good to see you," said Gallant.

"Henry, I'm glad I found you. Are you feeling ill?" asked Roberts, voicing his concern.

Gallant's face was unnaturally white and thin, and his sunken cheeks made his eyes bulge.

"I've never been better," said Gallant, furrowing his brow to emphasize that there was nothing more to be said on the subject.

"I've been worried about you. I just returned from deployment yesterday and learned of your predicament. I went to your old apartment, but they said you'd moved."

"John, it's good to see *you*. You look well. We moved out of the city. It got too expensive for us. Alaina has a job as a live-in tutor in the suburbs. I'm staying at the veteran's center temporarily."

"That's an outrage," said Roberts reaching toward his back pocket.

Gallant grabbed his arm and said, "I appreciate the gesture, John. That's not necessary. We're getting along just fine."

"No, Commodore. It's not right ..."

"Don't call me Commodore. I've been struck off."

"What! Gosh."

"I'm awaiting court-martial."

"Graves?"

Gallant nodded. He asked, "If you're not busy, why don't you come into the veteran's center and have a meal with me? At least you can get out of the rain."

"Sure."

They crossed the street and Gallant ushered Roberts to a table in the back. The center always had a hot meal available for veterans, and while it wasn't the finest cuisine, it stuck to the ribs and filled them up.

During the meal, Gallant hardly said a word and was embarrassed when he wolfed down his food before Roberts finished two mouthfuls.

Roberts asked, "What do you do here?"

"Oh, I help out with odd jobs around the building. A helpful pair of hands is always appreciated."

"It's a disgrace," said Roberts shaking his head. "You're working odd jobs after all you've done."

"It's not so bad. Once the court-martial is resolved, I'm sure everything will return to normal."

But Gallant's words sounded mushy as if there was no strength behind them.

"This is a fowl business."

Sunlight bounced off the glossy steel-and-glass fleet headquarters. Gallant recognized his distorted image reflected from the black monolith. Setting his jaw, he held Alaina's hand as he pushed open the heavy doors. As he stepped inside, the embedded sensors scanned his ID pin.

A guard pointed him toward a door on the far side of the lobby. He said to Alaina, "You'll have to wait in the lobby, Ma'am."

Alaina squeezed Gallant's hand and kissed him

on the cheek. "I'll be here, no matter what."

He smiled and started walking to the door.

He had only gone a few steps when the last person he wanted to see appeared at his side. Hooking her arm through his, Captain Julie Anne McCall led him toward the door.

She said with a seductive smile, "This way, Henry. I've been waiting for you."

Gallant didn't have eyes in the back of his head, but if he had, he would have witnessed the blistering stare Alaina burned into Julie Anne.

Entering the courtroom, Gallant was surprised at the gathering. Looking around the room, he didn't see Admiral Collingsworth. He had been counting on his support. He didn't see any representative from either the president or the secretary of defense. Gallant swallowed hard when he realized a dozen witnesses from his task force were also absent. What kind of defense could he offer under these conditions? His face burned with rage.

McCall smiled knowingly. She almost purred as she said, "Relax. Trust me."

Her words infuriated him as he gazed around the room and saw the court-martial flag flying.

With his black robe draped about him, the sour-faced judge gazed at his innocuous prisoner, seemingly unaware that he was holding court under unusual circumstances. An indictment rested on his desk with official seals and high-ranking signatures. Tags and attachments cluttered the dog-eared pages.

The senior officers that constituted the members of the court wore everyday uniforms. They seemed uninterested in the proceedings. A single prosecuting attorney sat at one table while Gallant's own defense counsel sat nearby. Surprisingly, no one else was present. Admiral Graves, his chief of staff, and Neumann's political hacks were missing. And there were no news reporters in the room.

The prosecutor had a small pointed nose and wispy whiskers. He stood up and held his hands close to his chest when he addressed the court. He spoke out of the corner of his mouth.

Gallant settled back in his chair. He expected a long windy opening speech by the judge and prosecutor followed by an equally long rebuttal by his defense counsel. He supposed that the trial would go on for many days and that he would be the subject on unrelenting attacking in the news media.

That was not the case.

The judge called the court to order. The clerk read an abbreviated version of the indictment. The prosecutor made an ambiguous opening remark. And then the defense counsel asked the court to rule on a point of order. The prosecutor did not demur. A moment later, the judge's gavel slammed down. All charges were dismissed.

The court-martial was over in five minutes.

"What just happened?" asked Gallant.

McCall said, "Never go into a critical meeting without knowing the outcome in advance."

"You mean this was all agreed to before I arrived."

"Of course."

"How?"

"President Kent and Admiral Collingsworth did some backroom bargaining with Gerome Neumann and Admiral Graves."

"Bargaining?"

"Yes. You were exonerated. But Graves retains the public illusion that he defeated Zzey at Ross."

"That's not right."

"Oh, Henry. You're adorable," laughed McCall heartily. "The line between right and wrong is not as clear in politics as the line between you and your enemy in battle."

"Graves will be able to play the hero and support Neumann for election."

"True. Your friends paid a high price for your freedom." She hooked her arm through his once more and led him back the way they came. "Go home to your devoted wife. You can return to the *Constellation* tomorrow."

CHAPTER 34

The Raid

Gallant sat in his cabin aboard the *Constellation*. The crew took it for granted that nothing had changed. But he had a new appreciation of what being captain of a warship meant. He spent a few hours wool-gathering before he sat at his desk and began writing a letter.

He submitted the letter to the President, via the Secretary of Defense.

> Mr. President,
>
> I am forwarding my report of the recent battle in the Ross System to Secretary Gilbert. I have included specific details to support my findings, but I would like to highlight a few of the most pressing issues in this letter.
>
> 1. As expected, the Titans used the Mar-

ines as bait to trap our relief fleet. Despite setbacks, our Sailors and Marines were equal to the challenge. They fought with determination and ferocity, and suffered unimagined loss, but our convoy was able to relieve the Marines. They now have strong defensive weapons and a fighter wing protecting Ross.

2. The Titans are likely to launch another mission against Ross as soon as they resupply and reinforced their fleet. It is therefore imperative for the United Planets to change the dynamics of the war by precipitating new fears in the Titan high command. While the UP occupies six stars between the Solar System and the Titans, the enemy inhabits nine stars systems surrounding the Gliese star.

3. I recommend that you direct Task Force 34 to conduct a hit-and-run attack on the Titan home-world, Gliese-Beta. That will compel the Titans to halt offensive operations and take a more defensive posture.

I await your orders.

Respectfully yours,
Henry Gallant
Henry Gallant, Commodore Task Force 34,

UPN

P.S. I've taken the liberty of forwarding a copy of the report to Admiral Collingsworth.

\-   the end.   -

FROM THE AUTHOR

I hope you enjoyed this book. I must confess, I'm proud of my characters and the story they tell. Gallant is bold and brave, with a strong sense of responsibility—qualities I admire. I would be grateful if you could post your comments and review on Amazon. Any feedback you provide on the new characters in the series would be helpful.

Regards,
H. Peter Alesso

For notification of future books, click the Follow button on the author page.

NEW SERIES

Commodore Henry Gallant
by H. Peter Alesso

SYNOPSIS

The Titan seek to expand their empire through Human genocide. They are creating an unstoppable war machine. Henry Gallant intends to change that with a bold strike at their home world.

But he can't succeed without help. An ancient race called the Chameleon may be the solution. Can he convince them to help?

Commodore Henry Gallant will lead Task Force 34 to the Chameleon's home world to make a deal.

Printed in Great Britain
by Amazon

79428337R00154